Moonscape

Mark Noble Space Adventure Book 1

Tony Harmsworth

Newsletter

Sign up for Tony's Reader Club newsletter for exclusive content and special offers.
Details can be found at the end of MOONSCAPE.

Copyrights and Thanks

Thanks to:

Wendy Harmsworth, Annika Lewinson-Morgan, Tim Major, & Wattpad

All rights reserved; no part of this publication may be reproduced or transmitted by any means, electronic, mechanical, photocopying or otherwise without the prior written permission of the author.

ISBN: 9798607639969

Copyright © A G Harmsworth 2020
Cover design by Brittany Wilson 2019

A G Harmsworth has asserted his moral rights.

Published by:
Harmsworth.net
Drumnadrochit
Inverness-shire
IV63 6XJ

1 Routine

[Note for non-British readers – Tony writes using UK English spelling, punctuation and grammar.]

The dust returned to the surface as if in slow motion. I'd kicked a cloud into the air as I turned towards the Earth which hung in the sky like a Christmas bauble.

The blue and white marbling was extraordinary. I lifted my gloved hand and covered the entire disk with my padded thumb.

With a single digit, I'd hidden all but twenty human beings in existence. Assuming my thumb was hiding the location of the ISS, perhaps I'd hidden those eight people too, leaving just the twelve of us on the surface of the moon, including the four in the Chinese habitat.

'Can you straighten it, Mark?' a voice called, intruding into my isolation.

'Two seconds, Roy,' I replied. I straightened the theodolite target pole, lining up the marks on the two gauges. 'Okay.'

I held the pole still and looked across at Roy. Between us was a one-kilometre crater named Timocharis Delta, one of the craters on the fringe of Mare Imbrium. We'd discovered it was relatively new, only a few thousand years old. A previous visit had indicated a magnetic core. Whatever had created Timocharis Delta must have been composed of iron. That wasn't unusual but warranted this closer examination.

In the distance I could see the wall of the main Timocharis crater, over thirty kilometres wide.

Behind Roy, a kilometre away from me, stood the six-wheel moon-buggy, our home during this six-day expedition. Ten kilometres to the west, Moonbase One awaited our return the day after tomorrow. We'd been carrying out surveys of craters east of Moonbase and were now on the homeward arm of the loop.

Back on Earth, our work on the moon's surface had initially been on the news almost every day but was now rarely mentioned. Real science wasn't as exciting as political scandals or soap stars' affairs. Very few of the general public would even know our names.

'Got that, Mark. Give me a few minutes to pack up and I'll drive around and collect you.'

'Roger that.'

That gave me at least thirty minutes to absorb the amazing location. Me, Mark Noble, standing on the surface of the moon, following in the footsteps of Neil Armstrong, metaphorically if not actually. The Apollo 11 landing site was, of course, an internationally protected area. No one was allowed to come within two hundred metres of it, owing to its historical significance.

I walked ten metres down the slight slope of the outer ring of the crater and turned to watch Roy. I could just make him out, walking towards the buggy. I leaned on the target device. It took little effort to stand on the moon, but there was a tendency to lean forward due to the mass of the backpack. Leaning on the target tripod helped my balance.

'Moonbase, I'm opening the access hatch.' Roy stood on the ladder and swung open the one-metre circular hatch towards the rear of the buggy. His tiny white figure filled the black hole in the buggy for a moment, then he pulled the hatch back into position.

I continued eastwards so that he could collect me en route to our planned overnight camping location.

'I'm in the buggy. Stowing the equipment and sealing the hatch, Moonbase.'

'Copy that, Roy,' came the tinny female response.

I plodded eastwards, kicking up dust with each step. 'Moonbase, Mark here. Surprisingly deep dust to the east of Timocharis Delta. At least ten centimetres here. Can't walk without kicking it up.'

'Acknowledge that, Mark,' said Crystal from Moonbase.

'On my way,' said Roy.

'Copy that,' said Crystal.

The buggy was on the move, heading eastwards to clear the crater rim. As I walked I looked down at the deepening dust. I'd not seen dust so thick during my three months at Moonbase.

'Odd. The dust is now at least twenty centimetres. It's halfway to my knees.'

'Normal here, just the usual couple of centimetres,' said Roy.

'Hi Mark, Blake here. Looking behind you, is there any change in the surface colouration as it gets deeper?' asked Blake Smith, Moonbase commander. I pictured Crystal sitting at the communication centre in the comdome with Blake leaning over her to speak.

I turned. It was becoming more difficult to move my feet. Not seriously, but I felt the resistance. 'No, Blake. Surface looks absolutely normal – the usual darker disturbed dust. You can see my footprints,' I said, sending him a digital image.

'Yes. Odd. Take care. Roy, you listening to this? Any change where you are?'

'I'm kicking up dust with the wheels, but nothing out of the ordinary,' replied Roy.

'Proceed with care,' said Blake.

I walked a few paces further and stopped. 'Roy, Blake. Dust up to my knees. Copy please.'

Blake cut in. *'Hold your position, Mark. Any deeper with you, Roy?'*

'Copy that, Mark. I've eased off to 4 k. Can't really see any change here,' replied Roy.

'Proceed with care, Roy. Mark, can you backtrack? I don't want you entering anything deeper.'

'Copy that. Backtracking.'

Soon I was back on the normal surface.

'Would it be better for you to follow my original tracks around the west side of Timocharis Delta, Roy?'

'Well, I'm halfway around now and no change in the surface.'

'Skirt well out into the plain to avoid whatever I've encountered.'

'Watch the speed, Roy. Slow to a crawl,' said Blake.

There was no doubt this was an unusual phenomenon. Before the Apollo missions, there'd been fears that there might be deep dust, so deep that the Apollo crafts might actually disappear into it and be lost forever. None of those fears had materialised.

'Have we encountered anything as deep as this?' I asked.

'No. Twelve centimetres in an area found by Apollo 14 at Fra Mauro,' said Blake. *'I'll mark the spot for a future investigation.'*

The buggy continued its journey eastwards and gradually began to turn south, but well beyond the original planned path. I could see very little dust being thrown up, but Roy was travelling extremely slowly. I looked at my O_2 gauge. Plenty.

'Halfway to Mark,' said Roy. *'Dust still normal.'*

'Copy that,' I said. Crystal acknowledged him too.

'I'm walking southwards so as to save Roy having to approach anywhere near that pool of dust,' I said, trudging slowly away from Timocharis Delta, trying to avoid adopting the bunny-hop gait when moving quickly on the surface.

'Copy that, Mark. Roy, skirt further south to be safe,' said Blake.

I walked a good forty metres southwards. The ground was absolutely solid, with just the usual one or two centimetres of fine, loose dust. I stopped and turned to watch the buggy's progress.

Roy was now some hundred metres east of Timocharis Delta and almost level with its southernmost tip. *'I'm turning westwards. Should be well south of Mark's dust pit,'* he said.

'Roger that, Roy. Proceed with care.'

The buggy was now approaching me head-on. It comprised a single lozenge-shaped cabin about four metres long and three metres wide. Inside there was plenty of headroom. It contained three bunks, cooking facilities, a chemical toilet and half a dozen seats. The structure sat on a raised chassis with prominent axles and six wheels with chunky tyres. Electric motors powered each axle independently and the hubs of the front two wheels contained additional motors to provide more traction if required. It was now pointing towards me, maybe fifty metres to the east of me.

'Do you think I'm far enough south of the pit, Mark?'
'Can't be sure, but probably,' I replied.
'Any change in depth?' asked Blake.
'Not so far.'
'Okay. Just stay cautious,' said Blake.
'Copy that.'
The buggy slowed to a crawl.
'Dust's thicker here,' said Roy.
'Okay. Stop,' said Blake.
'Stopped. Left front tyre at least twenty centimetres deep. Right front about ten centimetres. I can see wheels three and four are on normal ground. Think I should turn south again. Blake?' said Roy.
'Right. Turn south,' said Blake.
'Roger that.'

The front wheels turned to the right. The buggy started to move forward to starboard, beginning a turn southwards. I watched in horror as the entire cabin began to list to port.

'Oh, fuck!' said Roy.

The buggy slid forward and lurched sideways. I saw wheels spinning and dust flying as Roy slammed the drive into reverse.

'I've hit full reverse on all wheels!' shouted Roy.

All that happened was that the starboard wheels started to grip, but that swung the vehicle further to the south. In dreadful slow motion, the whole vehicle rolled onto its side, half the cabin and all of the port side wheels buried in the dust.

'Report!' said Blake.

'Buggy two's on its side. Here's some pics,' I said as I sent a series of images to Moonbase.

'On its port side. I'm half buried in dust,' said Roy.
'Stop all drives,' said Blake.

'Drives powered down,' said Roy.

'Seems to be just lying there. Not slipping deeper,' I said. What was most worrying was that the hatch was under the dust. A removable panel on the starboard side would give access, but releasing it involved all sorts of precautions, and even then it was cumbersome and was supposed to fall downwards. If I opened it, how could I lift it onto solid ground?

'No further movement,' said Roy.

I looked at my O_2 gauge. What had seemed plenty before now seemed far less adequate. We were in trouble.

2 Breathing

I did a quick conversion of my O_2 supply into minutes. A hundred. Not good, given the change of circumstances.

'Just looking at my O_2, Blake. Nominally a hundred minutes.'

'Right, Mark. We're having a look at your options. Will you head south for another fifty metres, then try to move east and see if that gets you around the dust pit? Great care now, and keep the walking to minimum energy. We're checking buggy one right now to give you an ETA,' said Blake.

'Roger. Heading south now,' I replied.

The ground remained perfectly solid, so I decided to change my heading to slightly east of south. Still no sign of deep dust.

The radio sprang back into life. *'Moonbase here. Can you tell us how you see your options, Mark?'* asked Crystal.

'Well, if I can't get around whatever this dust pit is, then I guess my only option is to go to minimum activity and await your arrival. If I can get to buggy two then I'll assess the situation and discuss with Roy whether to remove the access hatch. An immediate problem comes to mind – the hatch is awkward to manoeuvre, and we wouldn't want it to slide off into the dust.'

'Okay, Mark. I'm relaying that to a Moonbase-Earth conference discussing what's happened. Back to you soon,' said Crystal.

'Good job we weren't both inside this thing. That hatch can't be opened from inside,' said Roy.

'Right. We could still get through the back window, but I'd never be able to open that from outside in time on my own,' I said.

I reckoned I was fifty metres further south now so turned due east, one step at a time.

'Heading due east now. Ground still firm,' I said.

'Roger that,' said Crystal.

Once I was as far east as the buggy, I turned to face it. On its eastern side the three wheels were clear of the dust, as the buggy was resting at about 95° to the horizontal. The inner surface of the centre port-side wheel was just visible.

'Roy. You noticed any further movement since it slipped?'

'No. Nothing.'

'Mark, Roy – Blake here.'

'Go ahead, Blake.'

'Buggy one en route to you now. ETA eighty-two minutes if no obstructions encountered. That's really tight for time for you, Mark. What's your O_2 reading now?'

'Roughly eighty-eight.'

'NASA recommend dropping the psi to 3.8 shortly, but what we need to know first is whether or not you can reach your buggy. Head north towards it but keep east of its position to avoid the pit.'

I took a moment to use the Valsalva device to relieve an infuriating nose itch, then set off. 'Walking north now.'

'Good. If you can reach buggy two it opens up other options, but if you can't, buggy one will have to come south of Timocharis Delta to reach you, to be sure we don't run into the pit. If you can reach it then we can head straight around the north of the crater.'

'Copy that. Ground still firm. Only twenty metres from buggy,' I said.

I walked as economically as I could, keeping a close eye on the depth of dust.

'Still on firm ground. Buggy wheels directly in front of me, about two metres. I've poked the tripod into the dust in front of me and it's still firm. Wondering if there's a sharp ledge.'

'Baby steps, and keep poking,' said Blake.

'Careful, Mark,' said Roy from the buggy.

'Just over half a metre and the tripod is going down into the dust. Pushing. Yes, it's deep very quickly.'

'Great care,' said Blake.

'Can feel the edge with my boot now. There's a drop off, unlike my side of the pit where it deepened gradually. Explains why the buggy tipped so suddenly.'

'Nah. I was careless. Should've reversed away. Turning was crazy,' said Roy.

'O_2, Mark?' asked Blake.

'Seventy-one minutes.'

'We've had Jenny trying to take the panel off buggy three. Took her twelve minutes. So we need to think about the options.'

'Don't really want to open her up unnecessarily,' said Roy.

'No, but if buggy one hits a problem, Mark could soon see his O_2 diving.'

'Why don't I sit quietly for thirty minutes, conserve O_2 and see how buggy one's ETA has changed?' I said. 'If I'm going to open that panel, I've other problems than just the fixings.'

'Explain,' said Blake.

'Well… firstly, I have to step almost half a metre onto the tyre of port wheel one. What if that causes the buggy to roll further? Also, what if the tyre moves? There's nothing to support me unless I lean forward against the underside.'

'I see,' said Blake. 'Roy can lock the wheel so it doesn't move. What's your next move once you're on it?'

'Locked it,' said Roy.

'Thanks, Roy. I'll then have to jump up to grab the starboard side of the chassis. I don't think that will be too difficult given one sixth G, but if I did miss there's no certainty I won't drop into the dust. If I do get up to the chassis, I'll have to climb along it and lie on the side of the buggy to undo the fixings. I don't want to be attempting that on low psi or if I'm running low on O_2. It's now or never, really.'

'I'll go back to NASA on this. Sit quietly, Mark,' said Blake.

Moon suits are not particularly flexible, but I managed to get into a sitting position, facing the Earth. An almost cloudless Australia stared back at me. The gauge read sixty-seven minutes.

3 Patience

For a thousand, a million, perhaps even a billion years, it had been lying dormant in the dust of a rocky moon. It had no consciousness because there was no consciousness nearby. It was in deep hibernation. It sensed nothing, felt nothing, saw nothing and knew nothing.

But now it could sense a consciousness, just above its resting place. It sent out a tendril and encountered aluminium sheeting. The object was a vessel, lying still and silent in the dust. It became aware of thoughts nearby. It sensed some anxiety, not worry for itself, but for another entity elsewhere.

How could it get closer to the consciousness? It couldn't enter the creature without physical contact. Surrounding it was tightly packed dust. There was no atmosphere. The rocky moon was devoid of gases, but there was atmosphere inside the vessel.

It moved and twisted in the dust, trying to make better contact with the aluminium sheeting of its hollow prey.

Ah, contact. There was warmth. Well, warmer than the dust. There was something inside the vessel which was most certainly a living creature.

Now it was more fully awake, it sensed a second organism nearby, inactive, breathing shallowly. A long way off, vibrations were approaching.

Self-preservation took over. It needed to ensure it wasn't harmed by these things nor left behind when they passed by. Its primitive, existential need for contact with something live became all-encompassing.

Tendrils extended, sensing the skin of the vessel, it found a different material. A manufactured metal shaft. Solid. This wasn't hollow like the aluminium. It followed the length of the shaft and reached a much more complex object. The steel entered the centre of an alloy hub which was surrounded by a more pliable substance. It could move the surface of the substance and there was a minute gap between it and the other metallic alloy.

This was somewhere it could conceal itself. Compressing its tendril, it forced itself into the gap, squeezing itself to a thickness of only a micron or two, then straining and thrusting itself through the crevice and into a space between the alloy and the compound of the softer object.

Satisfied it was concealed safely, it waited. The vibrations it had sensed were still a long way off, but rapidly approaching. The two organisms were unmoving. The more distant one was still breathing, but shallowly. The other was behind the aluminium sheeting.

4 The Unforgiving Moon

'How's the oxygen now, Mark?' asked Blake.

'Eleven minutes – and I see buggy one on the horizon trailing a cloud of dust,' I said.

'Sounds good.'

'Hi, Mark?' said a female voice over the radio.

'Yes. That you, Linda?'

'Super-heroines to the rescue. I've got Mary with me. We can see you, Timocharis Delta and Roy's wreck. Will be there soon. Mary says she'll teach him to drive later,' said Linda.

Roy choked off a laugh. It was unlike him not to make an instant retort. I figured he was embarrassed.

The rescue buggy was approaching the top of the crater. One helpful aspect of the moon was that the horizon was so close – they'd reach me within a couple of minutes.

Roy's voice cut in. *'Great care as you come around the crater, Linda. We don't know if there are more of these pits.'*

'Yes. We must find out about this accumulation. Most unusual,' I said.

'We're taking care, Roy, but we accelerated when we got into your tracks. Coming around the crater now. Still following your tracks. Be there shortly.'

'Stop behind buggy two and I'll come aboard,' I said.

Mary said, *'I've suited up and am driving now, Linda's suiting up as I speak.'*

I fought my way to my feet. The difficulty of getting to a standing position was why we normally remained standing when wearing backpacks.

Buggy one came to a halt a couple of metres from buggy two and the dust pit. I made my way around to the door which was being opened for me. Within two minutes I was inside.

'Just for the record, Blake, I've three minutes air remaining. Think we should consider additional supplies mounted outside the buggies in future.'

'Yes, that's a bit tight, Mark.'

Within a few seconds, my backpack was recharged with power and oxygen. Linda and I climbed out of the hatch to assess buggy two.

'We can get a good fixing on the rear strut, Blake. Will it take the strain?' asked Linda.

'Send us an image and I'll forward to NASA,' said Blake.

'Image sent. Taking and sending more,' I said.

The buggy was lying almost on its side with all three starboard wheels in view. The front pair were rotated hard right, which was Roy's last action before it tumbled into the pit.

'If we attach the tow cable to the rear strut, that should pull it up if you keep a steady reverse drive running, Roy,' said Linda.

'I'm strapped in and ready,' replied Roy.

'Turn the buggy around, Mary, with the rear end towards us, please,' said Linda.

'Will do.'

Linda and I stood still, awaiting NASA's response and taking in the view of Earth hovering in the sky, so near yet so far. Buggy one backed up about forty metres and turned through 180°.

'I'll never tire of this view,' I said, looking at the Earth.

'No. Beautiful. So beautiful, you forget how unforgiving the moon can be,' said Linda. *'Three minutes!'*

'I could have extended that by further pressure reductions,' I said.

'Not by much. Suppose we'd broken down en route?'

'I'd have tried to open the emergency panel.'

'An emergency external supply is the answer. I'll do a report when you let me have your notes.'

'Right.'

'Reversing,' said Mary.

We moved to one side of buggy two to keep out of the way. Reversing lights flashed their warning and, if this had been inside the garage dome, we'd have heard loud beeps, once a second. The moon was a world of almost perfect silence, only broken by the odd sound travelling through my suit.

'That's it, Mary. Stop there and power down while we work on attachments,' said Linda.

'Linda?' said Blake.

'Receiving.'

'You've a go on attaching the cable to the rear strut, but NASA says, "no jerking".'

'Roger that, Blake.'

I opened the cubbyhole beneath buggy one and removed a four-metre, multi-strand steel cable about a centimetre thick. At each end it had a simple but heavy-duty snap hook. Linda ran her cable through the tow bar and attached her hook. Cautiously, I made my way towards the rear of our buggy. I felt the edge of the pit with my foot when I was still a metre short of reaching the strut.

'I'm at the pit edge,' I said.

'How about going around via the axle?' asked Linda.

'Your wheels still locked, Roy?'

'Roger that, Mark.'

I skirted the pit until I was adjacent to the rear axle. If I leaned forward, I'd be able to touch the wheel.

'Blake, no real choice here. I'm going to have to jump onto the wheel,' I said.

'No alternative?' asked Blake.

'Don't think so,' said Linda.

'Okay, Mark. Attach your end of the cable to your suit clip, then go for it.'

'Attached.'

I jumped. Pressurised gloves, even with silicon grips, were not the most suitable garments to try and get a grip on metal or the tyre material of the wheel. I began to slip, heard Linda shout out to be careful, and then managed to wedge my hand between the alloy hub of the wheel and the steel shaft.

I heaved myself forward – much easier than it sounds under a sixth of Earth gravity. Now I was secure, lying across the wheel. I could unclip myself and reach across to clip the cable to the strut, but it would leave me untethered.

Linda had anticipated the problem, and had already attached another cable to buggy one. She called out, *'Grab this second cable, Mark.'*

She threw it. The first attempt sailed over me and the hull of buggy two. *'Coo. Forgot my own strength,'* she said and laughed.

I managed to grab it on the second attempt, worked it back through my hand, clipped it to my suit and then unclipped the original cable to attach it to the strut.

Now I sat on the wheel and threw myself forward, Linda taking up the slack. I was safely back on *luna firma*.

Linda climbed back into her buggy and secured the hatch. I stood away from the action to report on what was happening.

Buggy one eased forward.

'Slack taken up,' I said. 'Begin low-rev reverse drive, Roy.'

He acknowledged the instruction, then the wheels began to spin.

'Okay, Mary. Slowly forward.'

The back end of buggy two began to rise out of the pit and, once the rear wheels were on firm ground, the whole vehicle tipped back to an upright position. In less than five minutes both vehicles were standing on the moon's surface.

I disconnected the cable and stowed it back on buggy one.

'That's your cable returned,' I said. 'I'm going to join Roy, take a rest break and after a meal we'll continue with the survey.'

I made my way around the buggy and found Roy had already opened the hatch. I climbed in gratefully. After we had repressurised it was a delight to slough off my suit.

'There's a no-go on that, Mark. NASA want all four of you back at Moonbase to check out that buggy,' said Blake.

'Looked fine to me,' I said.

'They want it checked,' said Blake.

'Okay, following the girls back,' said Roy.
'We'll try not to lose you,' said Linda.
'Dream on,' said Roy.

Both buggies headed round Timocharis Delta and then west towards base.

5 On The Move

Suddenly there was movement. Its hiding place was spinning, then rising, gripping the planetoid's surface. It sensed dust flying off in all directions as the object continued to rotate. There were five similar rotating objects, all heading in the same direction.

A few metres beyond, it sensed the movement of another of these self-propelled devices. There were now four living creatures nearby.

At last it might be able to fulfil its function. All it had to do was wait for the opportunity.

6 Moonbase

Even after several weeks, each time I drove into the garage dome I was surprised at its size – it was as large as a basketball arena.

The outer door closed and repressurising began. Once the klaxon gave the all-clear, all four of us exited our buggies.

The dome contained three six-wheel pressurised buggies and two open buggies similar to, but more sophisticated than, the original Apollo moon buggies. In fact, one was the buggy from Apollo 16, upgraded and reconditioned. It had powered up fine, but the batteries, seals and silicon components had all needed to be replaced. The lunar nights had taken their toll on a vehicle designed exclusively for daytime operations. After fifty years abandoned on the surface of the moon it was in remarkably good condition.

Mary and Roy began vacuuming the suits and the inside of the buggies. Moon dust was incredibly invasive and had to be thoroughly removed. Linda and I cleaned the exteriors. Mine promised to be a long job. The entire port side of the buggy was covered in dust and every nook and cranny would have to be sucked clean. I climbed the stepladder and began with the back, pushing the nozzle into every screw and rivet hole.

After emptying the cleaner for the fourth time, the cabin sections were complete. Now I began on the chassis, using a brush attachment to get into all the open areas along the drive shafts and around the motors. Roy joined me as we started on the wheels, me on the starboard side, him on the port side. Roy was one of those people who could see the funny side of anything. Amazing sense of humour. We got on incredibly well and had trained for our moon mission together.

I suppose the cleaning didn't really take too long, perhaps ninety minutes by the time I brushed off the last wheel on my side. I walked around the buggy to give Roy a hand and found him lying face down by the rear port wheel, shaking as if taking a fit. I ran straight over to him.

'Roy! You okay?' There was no response. I shook him, clicked on my personal intercom and shouted, 'Medic to garage dome. Man down!'

I turned Roy over and put him into the recovery position. His shaking stopped but now he wasn't breathing. I flipped him onto his back and began CPR.

I'd just completed the first thirty compressions and given the first two breaths when I was joined by Tosh – John MacIntosh, a medical doctor. He was the oldest of the Moonbase crew at just under fifty. He was stockily built with greying hair and craggy features.

He gave the remaining compressions and a couple of breaths. There was still no pulse.

'Continue, Mark,' he said and ran for the defibrillator pack.

By this time, everyone had arrived apart from Crystal, as it was prescribed that at least one person be in the communications centre at all times.

Eight times Tosh attempted to jump-start Roy's heart. We'd reached the end of our ability to rescue him. He lay there, his face pale, eyes glazed. He still appeared tall, young, strong and fit, except none of those things mattered any longer. He was dead.

Roy and I had passed through astronaut training together with geology doctorates and were inseparable at the Johnson Space Center. Now he was lying on the floor of the garage dome, dead.

I was stunned. I could do nothing. I sat cross-legged beside his lifeless body.

Blake and Linda carried a stretcher towards Roy. With Tosh's help, Blake lifted our fellow astronaut onto the orange litter and then onto a separate gurney. They wheeled him away.

Linda sat on the floor beside me and held my hand. It was a natural gesture as we'd been close since an affair during training.

'You were so close,' she said, putting an arm around my shoulders.

'Very. Right through training. Well, you were there too. I can't believe this has happened. What on Earth killed him?'

'Come on,' she said, 'let's get out of here. I'll make you some tea.'

'We hadn't finished cleaning the port wheels,' I said.

'No prob. I'll come back and do it later,' she said.

7 Violation

The beings were on a journey in their vessels. The concealment was good. It would not be discovered here. Around and around, the wheel turned. It felt the impact against myriad small stones, some bigger boulders and the smoothness of the dust. The lifeforms were unaware of its presence.

The rotations were slowing. The speed of the vessel reduced, then it stopped. The wheel no longer rotated. It was almost stationary.

Reaching out, it discovered a complex of buildings containing even more lifeforms. The vessels were entering them. A door closed and there was an inrush of gases filling the void.

A tendril eased itself out of its hiding place. Oxygen, nitrogen and traces of other gases. All harmless. This was the atmosphere these beings breathed – and there they were, leaving the confines of their vessels and moving around, passing almost within touching distance. It prepared for contact, oozing its way from the wheel and waiting on the alloy rim.

Several times, one of the bipeds passed nearby, climbing the sides of the vessel and sucking planetoid dust into a machine. How powerful was the suction? It would need to be ready to hold on to its location. The contents of the suction machine were being evacuated back onto the surface of the planetoid. It wouldn't want that to happen. It was desperately weak from its interminable hibernation.

It needed contact, and soon, if it were to survive. How long had it been dormant? How long waiting for a creature to approach? It didn't know. It seemed an age.

Another male began to clear the front wheel and axle of dust. When he reached the middle wheel, that would be the time to act. How would it attract attention? The creatures were communicating using sound waves. If it made a noise, more than one might approach. It needed a single being. There would likely be a struggle. It could be hurt and isolated. That wouldn't do. It needed some time alone with the creature to learn how to control it.

Sight would be the way to attract the being. It would have to make itself visible. Right now, it was an almost transparent gel, the size of one of the creature's fingers.

The being had finished cleaning the front wheel and moved towards its hiding place. With an effort of will, it turned blue and glowed. The creature stopped vacuuming and looked closely at it. The machine was still running. Could the motor be powerful enough to suck it off the wheel? The being pointed the nozzle at it.

Quick, make the glow pulsate. The being froze, got down onto his knees, laid the vacuum nozzle on the floor and peered at the wheel. Curiosity was a universal trait. One of its digits came near. Be ready, be ready, be ready. Might only be a single chance. Don't waste it. Ready, ready, ready. Contact!

In an instant, it was through the skin and racing towards the central nervous system. The creature shook its hand violently, trying to dislodge it, to no avail.

The being was preparing to shout. No, no, no. Mustn't let the being make a sound. Stop it! Stop it! Stopped it.

A violent tussle was taking place. The silenced creature was trying to attract attention, banging a clenched fist onto the ground, but the sound of the vacuum motor drowned it. What a fight. This being did not want to submit. As it shut down one limb, another swung into action, grasping for whatever was inside the mind. Head shaking, fists and legs kicking and struggling.

It needed to stop this. One of the others might see and come to the rescue. Had to stop these movements. Nerves. It found nerves in the body. Stimulation. Pain. Pain filled the creature from head to toe, but it was fighting, struggling, trying to evict it.

Gradually it overcame the frantic scrabbling and struggling. It stopped the heart, stopped the breathing. Still the creature shook and fought for survival. It admired the tenacity of the being, but it was, at last, winning the battle.

A second biped came into view, but the war was won. It had control at last. Shut it down. Hold it in stasis. The other creature was trying to restart the heart – was breathing into its facial opening. What a shame it wasn't stronger. It could have taken over a second creature there and then, but the fight had exhausted it. Needed rest.

What was that? The body jerked violently. The other beings were trying to electrocute it. Again, again, more thumping on the chest, more breathing into the facial opening. Hold the torso still. Keep the heart silent. Don't allow the oxygen to start the lungs again. The brain was still fighting. The creature knew it had been possessed. Hold it still. Quiet. No movement. The electric shocks stopped. Surreptitiously, it allowed some oxygen to circulate in the blood system. Keep the creature alive, but silent.

The body was lifted onto a trolley. It sensed movement. It was taken through another dome and into a third where it was left on the trolley and the creatures departed.

Now to take control of its prey.

8 Grief

Late the next morning, I strode into the common room and heard Tosh, saying, 'Well, I'm not doing it, Blake. And that's final!'

My entry seemed to cut everyone's tongues.

I looked around. Blake, our commander, forty, tall with rough-looking features and dark hair, was sitting at one of the workstations. Tosh, short and overweight, was leaning upon it with both hands curled into fists.

One of the sofas was occupied by Jenny, a diminutive, early-thirties, oriental woman from Korea, and Crystal, with whom she was having an open affair. Crystal was a slim, tall, jet-black woman of Ghanaian origin.

Linda was in the kitchen area making lunch for us both. Mary must be on communications duty. We all knew where Roy was – lying on the gurney in the medical cold room. His sense of fun was noticeably absent.

'What's up?' I asked, scanning their faces.

'Unimportant,' said Blake.

'Come off it! Stop pussyfooting around because he was my buddy. What's going on?'

'NASA want me to do a postmortem,' said Tosh, 'and I said I won't. There's a row brewing over my medical contract.'

'Why do we need a postmortem anyway?' asked Crystal. 'What happened, happened.'

'We've been through this,' said Blake, exasperation creeping into his voice. 'It's an unexplained death and must be checked out.'

'But how the hell am I going to be able to do that?' said Tosh. 'I've a small operating theatre area and some drugs. I don't have the ability to find out if it was a heart attack, a stroke or some neurological thing.'

'NASA say they'll give detailed instructions,' said Blake.

'Well I'm *not* doing it!' he shouted and stormed out.

I walked over to Linda and helped construct my chicken and salad sandwich.

'I finished cleaning the buggy's chassis and wheels,' she said quietly.

I thanked her and we both went to one of the sofas with our meals and coffees.

Conversation was subdued. I'd thought Blake might have followed Tosh to offer moral support, even though he patently had to put forward NASA's viewpoint on the death, but he just continued to pound his laptop. The rest of us kept a low profile. We knew NASA would probably compel Tosh to perform the procedure, but we also knew how he must feel. Although Roy was my "best buddy", he was well liked by us all. I wondered how I'd feel having to cut into my friend's body.

All of a sudden, the door burst open and Tosh re-entered, clearly distressed and furious. His cheeks glowed red with anger.

'Okay. Who's the fucking joker?' he shouted.

We all looked around with blank faces.

'What do you mean?' asked Blake.

'Some tosser is messing around. Where have you put Roy? He's gone!'

9 Control

Alone.

The other lifeforms had gone.

There was little light here, just the illumination from the adjacent dome through the circular window in the door. The ambient temperature was also much cooler in this location. Why was that?

What a fight this being was putting up. It was having a real struggle controlling the limbs. It hadn't expected such a duel. Not only that, but as it penetrated further into the being's mind, it found something it recognised. Something like itself buried within the brain. Two of them, in fact.

Had this creature already been taken over by its species in the past? No, this was different. This hadn't just arrived. This had grown with the creature from conception. Yet the similarities were amazing.

It struggled again. The hand moved. How could it keep control of this entity? If the being's colleagues saw a movement, they'd know there was something wrong. It explored the mind, began to understand the knowledge contained therein.

The being was called *human*. This wasn't the being's world. These creatures were explorers on this world. Learning about the planetoid. Some lived here, more lived in an orbiting station. Still more were in a large space station orbiting the neighbouring planet.

What a shock! It learned that the planet was home to billions of them, literally thousands of millions.

Plumbing the depths of the creature's memory, it found that others would examine the body to discover why it had died. It couldn't allow such an investigation. They might bury the body outside and that would be an end to it. Must not permit that. Must take control and hide. What else did the creature know about the possible turn of events? It dug deeper into the mind. The entity was called Roy. Roy could drive the vessels which they called buggies. It could escape using a buggy. Must get out of this room – now!

It explored the mind and brain, finding the locations of the areas which controlled sight, hearing, voice and, even more important, the limbs.

It forced Roy into a sitting position, the torso almost falling backwards off the gurney. Nothing about this would be easy.

The legs were clear of the ground. It shuffled forward, but the body tipped over and fell to the floor. Taking control of each limb, one at a time, it forced Roy up into a standing position. The battle still raged within, but control was vital... and needed quickly.

After numerous attempts, it managed to use the fingers to open the door and staggered, barely upright, to a platform in the centre of the room where it could lean for additional stability.

Tentatively, it probed further to learn more about the creature's balance. Devices in the human's ear were an important discovery. Fluid in the ear canals helped monitor balance when moving around. Feeling more confident, it left the medical room and found itself in a corridor. Which way? More probing of the mind. Right. Turn right. It walked along the corridor, occasionally needing to put out a hand against the wall to remain upright.

Was this the door? More probing. The being was lying to it, wanting it to take him through a different door, but it could hear beings in that room. The creature was trying to stop the escape, to lead it the wrong way. It forced the body to open a larger door at the end of the corridor.

It opened. Inside were the buggies, all prepared and facing the external door. Which one? The Roy thing wanted to use the machine called buggy two. Why? More pain for Roy. Buggy two was the least well charged.

It forced Roy into buggy three. Procedures. What was needed to get outside? Air. Evacuate the air. Shut the door first. Vacuum would be deadly to this being.

It felt the environment inside the buggy pressurise.

The maintenance dome depressurised. How did the door to the surface open? Extreme pain for Roy. It entered a code to open the outer door. The surface of the planetoid, which the being called the moon, stretched away to the horizon. It learned which controls steered the machine and pushed the accelerator. The vehicle shot forward.

It turned the steering device but had not appreciated that the three two-wheeled segments were articulated. It heard a grinding, tearing sound as it passed through the doorway. A tyre and wheel were damaged, but the machine was out of the dome now. It opened the throttle fully. The buggy shot forward towards the horizon.

Where could it hide? *How* could it hide? The buggy was leaving wheel tracks. It could be followed. There would be some time before the pursuit began. It probed the brain. It learned more. Roy could not hide the secrets the brain contained. Roy would help it. But Roy didn't want to help. The battle for control continued.

10 Search

They all looked at me.

'I haven't moved him!' I said.

'You just came in,' said Jenny. 'Where did you come from?'

'The geodome,' I protested.

'Stop arguing,' said Blake. 'Tosh. You're sure he's missing?'

'Of course I'm bloody sure. The sheet was lying beside the gurney, the door to the cold store open and the door to my surgery open too!'

'He can't have been dead,' said Crystal.

'I *know* when someone's dead!' said Tosh loudly.

'This isn't helping,' said Blake. 'We need to search the habitat. Two teams. Tosh, Jenny and Crystal; Linda, Mark and me. First of all, let's go to the surgery.'

All six of us left the common room, crossed the main corridor and entered Tosh's surgery and cold store.

The gurney was pushed against a cupboard and the green sheet which had been covering Roy lay in a crumpled heap on the floor.

'The door was open, you say?' asked Blake.

'Yes, and the surgery door. Some equipment was disturbed on my fixed gurney too, as if it had been pushed, rather than examined or anything. Just knocked out of the way.'

'Right. Tosh's group, turn left and check every single room and cupboard. Let Mary know as each area is examined. We'll turn right and check there. Meet up back in communications,' said Blake.

We split up and turned right into the central corridor.

The first door we encountered was to the biodome. We entered and walked along a hundred-foot tunnel. Some portholes opened onto the lunar surface. Outside, all appeared normal. We reached the biodome and Blake tapped in his access code.

The giant greenhouse-like dome opened up before us. A wall of shrubs and small trees greeted us. A unique haven of life on a dead world. We even had some chickens and, acquired recently, a beehive. The chickens were now kept in a coop as they could fly under moon gravity but made an absolute hash of it. They regularly flew into each other, us and the walls of the dome. When I first encountered the coop during my induction, Tosh told me about their erratic aerobatics and I laughed. He then said that there was nothing the slightest bit funny about a four-kilo cockerel flying straight at you with no brakes! Then we both laughed.

Almost a hundred metres in diameter, the biodome was even larger than the garage. It comprised panels of twenty-five-millimetre transparent aluminium-ceramic-composite glass strong enough to withstand micro-meteor impacts, and even larger meteors would likely skid off the surface – damaging it, yes, but possibly not breaking through unless they struck square on. Within the dome, two simian robots, so-called because of their agility, were equipped with repair patches in case something did get through. During tests, they were able to reach and seal a breach within four seconds, so the plants would be likely to survive.

During the two-week lunar night, the dome was illuminated by an array of lights which moved along rails fixed to the overhead struts. A small nuclear generator provided power.

We spread out, each following a different path through the foliage. There were five paths in total. Linda set out along the leftmost, Blake the centre, and me the rightmost. At the far side of the dome Linda and I came back along paths two and four, with Blake retracing his steps.

'Nothing?' Linda said.

Blake and I shook our heads.

'If he can't be found elsewhere, we can return and check the actual plant beds,' said Blake.

We reported in to Mary on the intercom and returned to the main corridor.

The next door was a storage area. It took barely two minutes to search.

Following that, we entered the atmosdome. It was a fairly open area and we searched it easily and quickly.

Next was the garage. I keyed in the code to open the door.

'No atmosphere in the garage,' said the computer, simultaneously sounding a short alarm.

The garage was only depressurised if one of the buggies was exiting. It then re-pressurised automatically when the outer door was clear of obstructions.

'Roy must be in there,' I said.

'We're stupid,' said Linda. 'Computer, locate Roy.'

'Roy is no longer in Moonbase. He left in buggy three,' said the computer.

'I can't believe none of us thought to do that straight away,' said Blake. 'Quick! Comdome!'

We all dashed along the corridor.

11 Probing

Pain was the answer. This Roy gave up his secrets to relieve pain. It controlled the nerves. Pain could be provided in many forms.

The tracks being left were a problem, but they weren't unique. Many tracks emerged from the… what was it called – a prod – Moonbase. Could they tell which our tracks were? The Roy thing said "no", but it was a lie. More than a prod this time – a sharp and continuous pain in the right hand. Ah, the damage to the rear wheel would make this buggy's tracks stand out.

Were there other Moonbases? Eventually the answer was positive. They were some distance away. A different nation… what are nations? A Chinese nation shared a base, with guest Russians. It was twenty hours driving away. What was the range of this buggy? About sixty hours. It recharged in sunlight while stationary. Was that a lie? Pain. More pain. No, it was the truth.

The Moonbase would speak to the other nations, so no point heading there. Get out of sight. Learn more. There were hills to the right. Get behind the hills and stop. Use pain to increase knowledge. What would happen if they caught this buggy? Find out. Dig into the Roy thing's mind. Get the information.

The buggy reached the hills, swung around behind them and travelled far enough to be concealed from view. It got Roy to shut down the buggy to conserve power and begin recharging. Now to dig deep into this mind and find a solution. It had time now, to learn.

12 EVA

We ran back, past the common room and into the comdome. Mary, a forty-year-old woman of Pakistani extraction, sat at the console. She was Blake's deputy.

'No sign of him?' she asked.

'Switch the monitor to the garage please, Mary,' I said with some urgency.

Mary hit a couple of buttons and the garage appeared on the main monitor. The camera automatically scanned to the left, back to the centre and then right. The outer door was open.

'Why's it not shut? There's nothing blocking it,' asked Mary.

'A buggy's gone,' I said.

'Yes. The computer says it's buggy three. But why's the door not closed?' said Blake.

Mary took the camera off auto and zoomed in to the doorway.

'Look,' said Linda. 'The bottom of the doorway has been damaged.'

'Close the door, Mary,' said Blake.

We watched as the door slid down on its runners until it was about half a metre from the bottom. Red lights flashed above the door and it retracted upwards.

'Buggy three must have impacted the door as it left,' said Blake.

'Don't be crazy! Roy's an expert at using those things,' said Linda.

'Well, it must've been him and it's definitely damaged,' said Blake. He reached over to the PA switch. 'Blake here, everyone to the comdome.'

Then he said to Mary, 'Get me Earth.'

The others joined us, and we all listened to Blake as he provided a report to NASA. It seemed bizarre, and it was obvious that those on Earth were sceptical about Tosh's examination of Roy.

At one point, Tosh grabbed the microphone from Blake and said, 'Don't tell me I made a mistake! I know when someone is alive or dead. Damn it, I'm a doctor!'

Blake snatched the microphone back from him, scowled and continued the conversation with NASA.

Once it was over, he said, 'Tosh, don't ever do that again during an official report. I know you know what you're doing, but, somehow, Roy has come back to life and we need to get him back here quickly, otherwise he could soon be dead.'

'He *was* dead!'

'Well, apparently not, Tosh, and if he's somehow got a reprieve, let's not mess up his recovery.'

'He damned well was!'

'Look. This isn't helping anyone,' I said. 'Let's find him and try to find out what happened.'

'Right. Okay,' said Tosh, resigning himself to the new situation.

'Linda. You and Mark suit up and see if you can repair the door. Tosh, you and Crystal go with them, fire up buggy one and get after Roy.'

'Crystal, take a seal tunnel with you,' I said. 'If Roy's ill he might not be capable of climbing into a suit, and you'll need to join the two buggies together.'

'Okay,' she replied.

The four of us headed to the small dome beside the garage to walk out onto the moon's surface. I wondered what was going on and where Roy was heading.

The Suit Dome was about twenty feet in diameter and contained our made-to-measure EVA suits. In the buggies, we used generic suits with limbs that could be shortened manually to fit the women and Tosh, the shorter members of our team.

We each clambered into our spacesuits. It wasn't a quick task, taking about half an hour, and the longer we took, the further Roy could have travelled in buggy three.

'Was three charged?' asked Linda.

'Yes, fully,' I said. 'It's interesting he didn't take buggy two. That was his favourite, but it won't be fully recharged yet.'

'He must be thinking straight to make that choice,' said Tosh.

'One should have a full charge,' said Crystal.

'Yes. Check and, if so, take that one,' I said.

Finally, we were all suited up, pressure-tested and fitted with full back-packs. The room depressurised and the door slid up on its runners. A puff of air preceded our exit, disturbing the dust around the entrance. Depressurisation never got down to 0 percent. There was always 2 or 3 percent remaining.

Linda led the way and we all bunny-hopped onto the surface of the moon, the strange gait which gave us the fastest speed in the low gravity.

We had to travel about twenty metres to get from the Suit Dome to the garage. Tosh and Crystal made their way straight to the equipment store and collected the portable tunnel which would allow them to join two buggies together if Roy was incapacitated.

Why had he run off like this? It made no sense. He must be ill or suffered a breakdown.

Linda and I examined the damage to the door. It was quite clear that the rear wheel of buggy three had side-swiped the door as it departed, having taken a turn to the right too soon. Driving the buggies was quite a skill, as they behaved like miniature articulated lorries. Roy, however, was the best driver of the lot, so for him to have collided with the door, he mustn't be in his right mind.

The runner had been impacted and bent, but it looked a simple matter to bend it back into position.

'Mark. NASA suggests you take the buggy. You're better trained on repairs. Can Tosh and Linda deal with the door repair?' asked Blake.

'Yes, no problem,' said Linda, seeing me nod.

'Might be good to have me there in case he's hurt,' said Tosh.

'Crystal and I can deal with the repair,' said Linda. *'It's not that difficult. Just need to straighten the runner.'*

Tosh and I climbed into buggy one, hurried through our checklist, shut the hatch and headed out onto the moon's surface.

'Strange,' said Blake. *'He's left the location device on, so he's not trying to hide from us. Buggy three seems to be parked behind Onizuka[1] Hill.'*

'Thought we might have to follow tracks,' said Tosh.

'We'll be there in around twenty-five minutes,' I said and pushed the pedal to the metal. My friend was dead and now was alive again. We needed to get to him quickly.

Buggy one shot across the surface, taking the most direct route to Onizuka Hill, dust thrown up by the wheels but settling quickly in the airless environment.

---

[1] Named for Ellison Onizuka, one of the fatalities on Challenger. In real life, he has both a crater and asteroid named after him. His personal oxygen supply had been turned on, meaning he might have been conscious throughout the descent. It is believed some of the crew wrote messages on their knee-pads. They were given to the families, but NASA made no comment.

13 Deceit

He lied by omission!

Its probing and questioning discovered that the wheel, no longer being square to the direction of travel, would leave a crooked track, but the Roy thing had deceived it by not revealing that they could be tracked electronically. The punishment was pain.

The location device was still active, but no longer after the flick of a switch.

The others would know where they were from what the Roy thing called "the tracking history".

The hill would not protect them from discovery and, by coming behind it, the buggy was now in a valley with a dead-end. Leaving by the only exit would make it immediately visible to its pursuers. It had lost the learning time it had hoped this would provide.

Its strategy had not been good. These creatures were well organised, not animals following instinct. If it took the buggy to the Chinese base, Moonbase would contact the Chinese and let them know there was a problem. It could hardly return to Moonbase, either.

Roy's mind told it there was a spaceship located about twenty minutes beyond Moonbase, but in completely the opposite direction. They would have to leave here and drive directly past Moonbase to the launch pad. The others would never allow that, and it realised it couldn't ever pilot the vessel by controlling Roy. The result could be its destruction.

It needed a different strategy. It put the Roy thing back into an unconscious state to concentrate on a plan, occasionally waking him to get information. The problem was that the easier the information was to obtain, the less useful it proved to be.

However, pain was an efficient incentive, so more was applied.

14 Found

Driving across the lunar plains was never smooth, but this well-worn route to Onizuka Hill was quite flat and I managed to maintain top velocity of about fifteen miles per hour.

'You should see Roy's buggy when you round the promontory,' said Blake.

'Copy that,' I said. Five minutes should do it.

'What if he's unresponsive when we get there?' asked Tosh.

'If we can't get any response, we'll have to fit the tunnel.'

'You ever used one before?'

'Not in a real situation. Trained to do it back on Earth, of course. And Crystal and I tested the system in zero atmosphere in the garage about three weeks ago. Getting a good seal on the second vehicle isn't easy. You've not used one?'

'No. Wasn't on the curriculum for my first stint up here and two-timers only trained on new equipment.'

'Not a problem, Tosh. I'll keep you right.'

I eased off as we approached the extended left slope of the hill. The distorted right track of buggy three was easy to follow, now that there were fewer tracks on the surface.

Abruptly, the track veered to the right, climbing the slope.

'Strange,' I said. 'Look how Roy's approached the slope. It would have taken the tilt of the buggy to at least twenty percent. Almost as if he didn't care if he tipped it over.'

'Why would he do that, Mark?'

'Don't know. He'd definitely have got warning lights. Why has he done any of this? You're the doctor. You tell me.'

'Well, I'm assuming he's suffered some sort of trauma. His fit in the garage indicates that. Looked to me like the central nervous system playing up. Maybe he's got a cerebral problem of some description.'

'Gone mad?'

'I wouldn't put it like that, but he seems to have suffered some aberration. Nothing else would explain why he'd leave the safety of Moonbase and set off in the buggy.'

'Is he trying to kill himself or something?'

'It's a possibility we mustn't ignore. He might even try to harm us for attempting to help him. Keep that in mind.'

I stared at Tosh in shock. Would Roy do something like that? 'I will.'

We were now travelling at about four miles per hour. I skirted around the promontory Roy had driven straight across.

'You can kill yourself pretty easily and painlessly in these things,' I said.

'What, the euthanasia valve?' Tosh said, tapping the circular red spigot at the upper right of the front console.

We all knew about it. Turning it would allow the buggy's atmosphere to drain off extremely slowly, causing unconsciousness first, followed by a painless death a few minutes later.

'Yes. Let's hope that wasn't why he came out here,' I said.

I slowed still further as we turned to the right. There, in the distance, was buggy three, facing away from us and unmoving.

'Blake. We have buggy three in sight,' I reported.

'Copy that, Mark. By the way, the GPS signal cut out about fifteen minutes ago. A bit late if he's trying to hide from us. Any ideas?'

'No,' said Tosh. 'All I can think is that it's some sort of mental aberration, brought on by the fit he suffered in the garage. He passed his weekly medical just two days ago. Everything was fine.'

'Okay. Caution on the approach, Mark.'

'Copy that,' I said.

'Blake. I'm really pissed off with NASA thinking I messed up. I expect you to put them straight,' said Tosh.

'They're listening in to this, Tosh.'

We looked at each other and laughed.

'Damn it. Trust me to put my foot in it!' said Tosh.

'Don't worry about it. When we've got him back to Moonbase, I'm sure we'll discover what happened.'

We moved slowly alongside the slope of Onizuka. As was the case with many old lunar hills, the slope met the flat plain quite sharply. Other than centuries of dust which had rolled down the hill, there was very little blending of the hill with the plain.

I eased us to a stop alongside, but about three metres away from, buggy three.

'Hi. Roy. Mark here. We're alongside you,' I said on the communication system.

Blake had been trying to contact Roy during our entire trip to no avail, but I wondered if the voice of a friend, now so close, would get a reaction.

Nothing.

We could see into the driving area. Roy was sitting in the left seat. There was no sign of any movement.

'Blake. We can see him. Not moving,' I said.

'I can see his chest rising and falling. Very slowly, but he's definitely alive,' said Tosh, handing the binoculars to me.

I focused on my friend's chest. There was no doubt that he was breathing. He was still in the sweatshirt top he'd been wearing on the day of his fit. His eyes were closed – at least, the one I could see from my position.

'Where there's life, there's hope,' said Blake.

'Here. Flash this at his face,' I said, passing Tosh a high-power torch from the accessories box on my side of the vehicle.

Tosh aimed the torch at Roy's face and flashed it several times.

'No response to the flashlight,' said Tosh.

'Okay,' I said, 'I'm getting out. I'll bang on the screen and see if he reacts to that.'

'Sounds sensible,' said Blake. *'Take care, now. Full EVA procedures, please.'*

I began the checklist.

15 Learning Process

Another buggy was approaching. It sensed the vibrations. The machine slowed and parked to the left. It kept the Roy thing in a sleeping state, although the brain was still active. It delved deep into the human's past, its education and knowledge.

From the Roy thing's brain, it learned that the others would enter its buggy and Roy would be transported back to the medical facility at Moonbase. If it could keep Roy unconscious, but still breathing, they would not cut into him.

A light flashed on Roy's face. The creatures in the other buggy were trying to discover if he was alive or dead. It increased the depth of Roy's breathing. The flashing stopped.

All was still again. It continued its learning process and waited for developments.

16 Making Connections

I removed my full EVA suit and put on the more flexible suit we usually used when working from the buggies. It was lighter and not as bulky.

We checked each other's seals and I depressurised the buggy. The door swung out and backwards, automatically securing itself against a fitting on the outside of the vehicle. Tosh slid the ladder down from below the entrance platform and I was soon on the surface. He passed me a telescopic rod, similar to the theodolite target pole I had used yesterday at Timocharis Delta.

I looked up at the cockpit of buggy three. Roy was sitting motionless as if asleep. I tapped three times with the pole on the glass. I could only hear the sound passing down the brush handle and through my suit, but from inside the buggy the sound would certainly be noticeable.

'Any reaction to that?' I asked Tosh, who was watching Roy's face with the binoculars.

'No. Nothing.'

I tried twice more and still no reaction.

'Mark.'

'Yes, Blake?'

'You've a go to install the tunnel. Let me know when your part is in place, before attaching it to buggy three.'

'Copy that, Blake. We'll need to turn the vehicle first,' I said. 'Tosh. Can you retract the ladder and shut the hatch first please, then swing a wide circle and come back facing the other way? I'll tell you when to stop.'

'No problem,' Tosh replied.

I walked away from the buggy to ensure I was out of its path, especially as Tosh wasn't proficient with these vehicles. He'd been trained on them, of course, but that wasn't the same as using them on a daily basis.

'Ladder stowed and door closed,' Tosh reported about five minutes later. *'Powering up.'*

'Copy that,' said Blake.

'I'm standing clear,' I said.

Buggy one turned to the left and drove onto the plain between the hills, taking a large sweep around before heading back to buggy three. I moved to the back of Roy's vehicle so that Tosh could see me.

'Stay about two metres from the vehicle, Tosh.'
'Copy that.'
I waved him forward until the vehicles' doors were opposite each other.
'Forward another ten centimetres.'
'Copy that.'
'Slow. Too far. Creep back. Stop.'
'Okay?'
'That's perfect, Tosh. Power down and open up.'
'Will do.'
I walked back to the front of Roy's buggy. He hadn't moved position. It certainly looked as if he was asleep or unconscious.

I climbed the ladder and Tosh passed me the tunnel portal. It was a flexible ring which fitted to the outside of the doorway, clear of the top of the ladder. Firstly, we had to unclip the hatch so that the portal covered not only the doorway, but also the hatch hinges. With Tosh's help, I fitted the portal in about five minutes, then sealed it with quick-cure sealant.

The tunnel design was rather clever. You had to put the two portals in place so that there was a seal outside each buggy. The portals were then joined with a platform which attached to the bottom lip of each portal. The flexible tunnel was 1.3 metres in diameter and had to be fixed, from the inside, to each portal. The bridge itself was underneath the tunnel, providing external support. It would never have worked except for the moon's sixth gravity.

It took almost an hour to complete the connection.

'Right, Blake. Tunnel and portals connected. Can I pressurise?'
'Copy that, Mark. Slowly.'
'By the book,' I said.

I opened our pressurisation valve and we watched the needle climb to point five of an atmosphere.

'Selena. How's the pressure holding?'

'Very steady, Mark,' answered the computer.

'Increasing to point eight,' I said.

A couple of minutes later Selena confirmed the pressure was holding, meaning there were no leaks.

'Blake, that's us set up.'

'All pressure checks within tolerances?'

'No loss at all. Selena says the seals are perfect.'

'Okay, keep your pressure suits on.'

'Of course.'

'Right. You have a go to open buggy three,' said Blake.

I made my way, on my hands and knees, across the bridge. It wobbled unnervingly in the middle, but that was an expected effect.

I reached the other door. I now had to keep in mind that Roy was not well. If he was trying to hide away, would he be dangerous? He might not appreciate being rescued.

Full of apprehension, I put my gloved hand into the socket and turned the lever.

17 Caution

It sensed movement outside and an object impacted the window. One of the creatures was trying to attract Roy's attention. Keeping the Roy thing in an unconscious state was becoming easier and it could do that while exploring his knowledge, trying to discover what was likely to happen next.

The others would attach some unit to the buggy and gain access. They would then examine Roy. It would have to keep him silent and passive. By doing that, the others would probably return him to Moonbase and keep him in a section of a place called surgery, for humans who were unwell.

All of this would give it time to discover how to control the Roy thing, perhaps even to be accepted by the others. Hibernation in the moon dust had depleted all of its reserves. Now it was growing in strength all the time, feeding on the metabolic system of the host. If it could fully control Roy, the opportunity would arise to take over a second human.

Caution was necessary. There must be no indication of threat given to the others or captivity would be more likely and suspicion of Roy would come to the fore.

Patience would be essential. There were fantastic opportunities for a being such as it. Take over both moonbases, then the orbital platform, then the space station in orbit around the blue planet and, finally, billions of subjects would be laid before it on the planet itself.

Progress may be slow now, but the rewards would be immense.

18 Rescue

The handle stopped in the safety position as the door detected the difference in pressure between the tunnel, at point eight of an atmosphere, and the buggy at one atmosphere.

'Mark. The pressure is rising,' said Selena.

'Selena. Allow it to rise. Tell me when it reaches point nine,' I said.

The safety position of the door handle allowed atmosphere to bleed outwards. It wasn't welcome in this situation. When it got to point nine, I'd force the handle past the safety stop point. Once I had the door open, I could get the computer in buggy three to reduce its pressure. I wouldn't want a sudden drop of more than ten percent with Roy not wearing a pressure suit, but a full atmosphere inside the tunnel would exceed safety levels. If the seals burst it would kill Roy.

'Blake. This needs reporting to NASA. There should be a way to contact the computer from outside or for the computers to contact each other in this situation.'

'Copy that, Mark. I'll ensure it is in the report. If we had that ability, we might have been able to stop buggy three in its tracks earlier,' Blake replied.

'Yes. If buggy three had been facing the opposite way, I'd have had to drag it around so that we could line up the hatches. Would not have been easy because it was powered down and the brakes were on.'

'Mark. Pressure passing point nine,' said Selena.

'Selena. Drop back to point eight as soon as I open the door.'

'Confirmed Mark. I'll reduce pressure to point eight when you open the door.'

I braced myself against the door, pressed the handle inwards and turned. The door pushed hard against me as the air pressure tried to equalise.

'Cavor. Reduce air pressure to point eight.'

'I read you, Mark. Reducing air pressure to point eight,' said the computer inside buggy three.

I swung the door outwards and entered the buggy. Roy hadn't moved.

'Okay, Tosh. Come through.'

'On my way. Don't touch him.'

I stood and surveyed the interior of the buggy. It looked absolutely normal.

Tosh made his way past me towards Roy. He removed a glove and pressed his fingers to Roy's neck.

'Slower than normal pulse, just thirty.'

Something seemed to puzzle him. He changed his position and checked again. 'That's odd. His pulse has increased to sixty. It was almost instantaneous. How the hell can that be?'

'You're sure about the first reading?' asked Blake.

'No. I made it up for fun! What do you think? Of course I'm bloody sure!'

'Sorry, Tosh. Had to ask.'

'It's stabilised at sixty. Breathing is a bit odd. Deeper than you'd expect for someone unconscious.'

Tosh suddenly stood back.

'That's crazy! As soon as I mentioned his breathing being oddly deep, it immediately changed to relatively normal,' said Tosh.

'Maybe he's coming around,' I said.

'No. I mean relatively normal for an unconscious person. This is weird. I mentioned his pulse and it came back to normal and the same with his breathing. We need to get him back to the lab. Something really freaky is going on here.'

'Okay, Tosh, Mark. Let's get him back quickly. Crystal and Linda are on their way to you. Disconnect the tunnel and get back here as quick as you can. One of the them will recover buggy one.'

'Copy that, Blake.'

'But no safety shortcuts.'

'Of course not,' I said. On the moon, taking safety shortcuts was a quick way to end up dead.

I lowered the airtight partition behind the cockpit to seal the area where Tosh and Roy were, then crawled along the tunnel. 'Cavor. Drop aft pressure to zero. Selena, drop pressure to zero.'

'Dropping aft pressure to zero, Mark,' said Cavor.

'Dropping pressure to zero, Mark,' repeated Selena.

The tunnel material sagged as pressure reduced. I detached it from buggy one and crawled backwards along it, then separated it from buggy three and stowed it. Finally, I yanked on the bridge platform, telescoped it, stored it, backed into buggy three, closed the door and repressurised. The portals would stay in place until we returned to the garage. Crystal or Linda would stow the bridge supports.

As soon as Cavor had the atmosphere back to one, matching the cockpit pressure, I lifted the hinged partition back to the ceiling to stow it. The ability to pressurise the cockpit separately was designed to allow someone to nip in and out to take readings or measurements without requiring all the astronauts to be in pressure suits.

'How is he now?' I asked as I removed my suit.

'No change. It's as if he's catatonic, but the muscles and limbs are completely relaxed. Extremely odd.'

'Do you think he'll be okay?'

'Really can't say. He was *dead* twenty-four hours ago. I'll lay off the predictions until I can do a proper examination.'

Carefully, we lifted Roy out of the driving seat and laid him on one of the bunks.

I switched on the buggy com-system. 'We're returning to Moonbase, Blake,' I said.

'Copy that. You'll pass the girls en route.'

'Powering up.'

'Copy that,' said Mary. I guessed Blake had left the comdome now we were on our way back.

I drove forward then swung around behind buggy one and headed back towards Moonbase. The damaged wheel caused the vehicle to pull to the right. As we came around the end of Onizuka Hill, buggy two was approaching.

'Hi, you two. Left you to stow the bridge supports,' I said over the radio.

'Okay, don't mind tidying up after you. See you later,' said Linda.

Tosh sat on the side of Roy's bunk, regularly checking his pulse and breathing, and shining a light into his eyes.

'His pupils are reacting normally,' said Tosh, 'but his blood pressure reacted to my voice, just like his breathing and pulse did. It was 95/50 and I whispered, "That's strange," and it jumped to 120/65, which is normal for Roy. What on Earth is going on?'

'We're not on Earth, Tosh!'

He laughed and said, 'Ha. "What on Luna is going on?" doesn't have the same ring to it.'

'No,' I agreed.

'Bloody odd, though. Feels creepy.'

I was hungry, and we couldn't help Roy until we were back at Moonbase. I opened the throttle and now we were on the smooth, well-used surface, the buggy leapt forward. Moonbase was in sight, the domes just appearing over the horizon.

19 Hiding

The pressure was dropping. The buggy seemed to be trying to maintain it. Another creature was at the door. Suddenly there was a outrush of air and the door opened. The pressure steadied at a lower level. A creature in a pressure suit entered. His name was Mark, a friend of the Roy thing. One of those who tried to help Roy when it took him over. Roy had a special connection with this friend. Roy tried to hide the relationship, but it dug, applied pain and was soon in possession of the truth.

Another creature entered. He was the doctor and he was approaching Roy.

It rechecked its control of Roy's vital signs. Keep the breathing steady. Ensure a smooth flow of blood.

The doctor removed a glove and pressed fingers against the Roy thing's neck. The connection of another creature fired up impulses in it. The desire to replicate, a compulsion to split and enter the second being. It could do it, but its knowledge told it to resist. Controlling a second creature now could cause it problems. Firstly, it must learn how to manipulate its host in such a way that it would be indistinguishable from the original being. So far it had made a real mess of that objective.

The doctor voiced concern at the pulse being slow. The pulse was caused by the heart. It raised the frequency of the heartbeats. Again, the doctor was concerned about the deep breathing. It had made Roy breathe deeply so as to appear alive to an observer, but this was too deep for a person who should seem to be asleep. It adjusted the rate and depth. The doctor seemed satisfied now, but also suspicious.

They closed off this section of the buggy. The rear section depressurised, and the friend of Roy dismantled the connection between the two vehicles.

The door was closed. It must now keep the Roy thing still. The second creature assisted the doctor to move Roy into a prone position. Once more, the sweetness of the connection of skin with skin. No. Resist the temptation.

Gain strength. The time will come. Do nothing rash. Wait and watch and learn.

After a short while they were on the move.

20 Examination

Back in the garage, Tosh and Blake wheeled Roy off to the surgery and Linda helped me with the buggies. She held the ladder as I cut the portal away from buggy one.

'You know, it would be a much better system if these portals were permanently fixed to the buggies,' she said.

'They will be if new ones are sent up.'

'Really?'

'Yes, but I doubt we'll still be here when they arrive. They reckon the life expectancy of these vehicles is ten years or more.'

I put the portal to one side, along with the other one. At some point, one of us would clean the sealant off the flush side so that it could be used again.

'Shame we can't leave them attached,' I said.

'The sealant, apparently.'

'Yes, it gets brittle remarkably quickly. Would have been pretty damn fatal for Roy if a seal had gone during the rescue.'

'What do you think is wrong with him?'

'No idea. On the way back, Tosh did a number of simple tests and got some strange cardiovascular results,' I said.

'Selena. Power down and recharge,' said Linda.

'Powering down and recharging, Linda,' said Selena.

I opened buggy two, removed the three tunnel support struts, and stowed them with the tunnel.

'Four portals left. I'll order a couple of replacements.'

'How about sealant?' asked Linda, who was now tidying buggy two.

I looked at buggy three's damaged wheel. 'I think the rim has had it. I'll change the wheel later and check the stock of sealant.'

'Fancy a coffee?'

'That'd be nice, but let's check in with Tosh first. Bedford, power down and recharge,' she said.

'Powering down and recharging, Linda,' said Bedford. The buggy computers were all named after characters from the film *The First Men In The Moon*, an H.G. Wells novel.

We left the garage and headed for the surgery. 'Tosh, you there?' I said into the intercom.

'Yes. Please come in.'

Linda and I entered the surgery.

'I've got him through here,' said Tosh, leading the way to a small room off the main surgery. 'Don't react to anything I say in there.'

'Why? Is there a change?' I asked.

'Yes. Too many changes! Now watch for my hand signals.'

'Hand signals?' asked Linda.

'You'll see what I mean.'

We stood beside the bed, looking down at Roy, who had an ECG attached, as well as a drip feed and a blood pressure monitor.

Tosh pointed at the blood pressure monitor, which showed 120/65. He then put his finger to his lips to request silence.

'He seems okay, but I'd like to see the diastolic at 60,' he said and pointed at the machine.

I couldn't believe my eyes. It dropped 64,63,62,61,60 over about two or three seconds.

Tosh gave the signal for silence again.

'I suppose 65 would be okay if we had the pulse up to 70,' he said and pointed at the device.

The pulse rate increased to 70 and diastolic returned to 65.

'Perhaps better as it was,' he said, and we watched the digital read-out return to 120/65 and a pulse of 60. Incredible.

'Let's leave him to rest,' Tosh said and guided us back to the main surgery.

'What's going on?' Linda and I asked, almost in unison.

'I don't know, but whatever I want Roy's body to do, it does within a few seconds of me saying it. How can any unconscious person achieve that? When I called it "freaky" on the way back to Moonbase, I wasn't joking. Whatever is happening to him is eerie. It's as if he is hearing me, but even then, I don't know anyone who can control their automatic bodily functions like that.'

'Sounds like he's possessed,' said Linda.

'Don't! It's spooky enough as it is without bringing in the paranormal,' said Tosh.

'Could it be some drug-induced thing? Did he inhale something odd when he was cleaning the buggy wheels, and it's affected him... or infected him?' I asked.

'Well, we might have some evidence to support that theory. Come over to the comdome and I'll show you. Jenny and Blake have been working on a video of the time when he had the fit. Computer, alert me if the ward door opens.'

'I'll alert you if the ward door opens, John,' said the computer.

We crossed the corridor and entered the comdome, where Jenny and Blake were studying a monitor and Crystal and Mary were sitting nearby. They looked around as we came in.

'We've managed to enhance it a little,' said Jenny.

We all peered over her shoulder. Blake stood back to give us some room.

The monitor showed a freeze frame of Roy in the process of vacuuming the front port wheel of buggy two.

'Watching?' asked Jenny. When we made noises of affirmation, she said, 'Normal speed first.'

We watched Roy finish cleaning starboard wheel one, then move on to the central wheel. He seemed about to start but then he stopped, looked closely at the rim of the wheel, brought the vacuum nozzle around, then stopped again and kneeled down. He laid the vacuum down and peered at the rim, reached out as if to touch something. Then, instantly, he was writhing around on the floor.

'What did he see?' I asked.

'We don't know,' said Blake.

'Now watch in slo-mo,' said Jenny.

She ran it back until Roy turned to the second wheel.

'He definitely saw something on the wheel,' she said, 'but he appeared to intend to vacuum it anyway. Then it seemed to become of greater interest – he stopped and that's when he kneeled.'

Jenny changed the playback to ultra slo-mo and zoomed in on the wheel.

It was extremely pixelated, but there was no doubt that there was something pulsating on the rim. It seemed to me that it had a slight bluish colour. The moment Roy's finger made contact, it vanished completely, and then Roy began his fit, or whatever it was.

'He definitely saw something unusual,' I said.

'For sure, but what?' asked Blake.

'I checked his right hand and there's no sign of any wound, puncture, mark or anything unusual on any of his fingers or any part of his hand,' said Tosh.

'Do you think it's inside him?' I asked.

'Oh, don't,' said Linda. 'You think we might be in danger?'

'It might be a one-off,' said Blake.

'But we have to vac those wheels every day. It could happen again, to any of us,' said Linda.

'Okay. In future, use airtight suits when vacuuming,' said Blake.

'I'm going to give him a CT scan after the sleep period. I should have a couple of the team with me in case it's a parasite and decides to jump host,' said Tosh.

'Oh, Christ! No,' said Linda.

'Wait a minute,' said Crystal. 'This means there's life on the moon. That's rather a huge discovery.'

'If it is life, yes. We need to isolate it and find out if it's alive, and we also need to put Roy into quarantine,' said Blake.

'The ward door is airtight,' said Tosh.

'What about ventilation vents, et cetera?' asked Crystal.

'I've got the air supply on self-contained setting. Computer, lock the ward door.'

'Locking the ward door, John,' said the computer.

'Use airtight suits while you're treating him,' said Blake.

'I don't have an airlock, though.'

'So something could get out as you enter?' asked Linda. She sidled up to me. She was really rattled. Most unlike her.

'Yes,' Blake replied, 'but hey, I don't think we're dealing with a xenomorph here.'

'That's a nice thought,' said Mary. 'They'll make a film about us.'

'Xenomorph? What's that? You don't mean the thing from *Alien*?' asked Linda, with growing apprehension.

'Yes, but it's tiny. Nevertheless, let's not underestimate what's happened, either,' said Tosh. 'If it's alive it could be dangerous. Whatever he touched was bigger than bacteria.'

'This is getting frightening,' said Linda. I put my arm around her shoulder.

'You can guess what's going to happen,' said Tosh.

'What? What's going to happen?' asked Linda, beginning to get hyper. I'd never seen her like this before.

'Tosh is hinting that the entire base will be put into quarantine,' said Blake.

'We'll be in isolation. How long for?' she asked. I felt her trembling.

'Come on, Linda. Calm down,' I whispered.

'It's a possibility,' said Tosh. 'They quarantined the first three Apollo missions in case they brought anything back.'

'But nothing can live on the moon. *Nothing!*' she said.

'It looks as if you're wrong, Linda. This entity must have come from somewhere,' said Crystal.

I squeezed Linda's shoulder to try to get her to relax.

'I wish I could get an extremely large gin and tonic,' she said and gave a nervous laugh. Her hand sought out mine.

'We're all getting ahead of ourselves,' said Jenny. 'Do you lot want to clear out? I've got daily reports to send.'

'You all right on your own?' asked Crystal.

'Don't *you* start. I'm not afraid of being alone. Okay?' Jenny said loudly.

'Forgive me for breathing,' said Crystal, scowling at her partner.

'I want to watch that video again,' said Tosh. 'Can you set it up in slo-mo for me, Jenny?'

'I've transferred the file to monitor three. You can play with it over there. I really need to get my reports sent,' said Jenny.

The rest of us left the comdome and headed to the common room. I cooked some tuna with Mediterranean rice for myself and Linda. We snuggled on the sofa and ate from laptrays. I was worried about Roy. The chance of him being infected with something was serious for all of us. We drank hot chocolate, and everyone started to drift away for the sleep period. We tried to run on a twenty-four-hour clock, because each lunar day was four weeks, two brilliantly lit and two pitch black. Normal-length 'days' helped maintain our body clocks.

'I'm off to bed, Linda. That was a long, hard day,' I said.

'Can I come?' she asked in a small voice. She really was taking this badly. 'Just for some comfort,' she added. 'I'd rather not be alone.'

I stood, offering my hand, and we headed for my room. It wouldn't be the first time, and it wasn't unwelcome.

21 A Patient Patient

Several groups of humans came to visit. There were two distinct types. Exploration of the Roy thing's mind told it they were male and female. They all showed genuine concern for Roy. Now that it had learned the language, its learning curve was improving rapidly. It needed to use pain much less often and discovered it could control the movement of fingers and toes freely. Occasionally, Roy resisted, but he could no longer prevent its actions.

Once the room was free of others, it opened Roy's eyes and moved his hands, learning how to grasp, how to see, how to move the head from side to side. Roy could no longer stop it, couldn't even come close.

It was prevented from standing and walking by the equipment attached to Roy's body. It could remove the sensors, of course, but it was learning about the sort of treatment it would be likely to receive. It decided not to do anything which would be seen as unusual.

The last group to visit had been the doctor, the friend called Mark and a female named Linda. It learned that changing the blood pressure, breathing and heart rate puzzled them. It wouldn't do that again. Conforming offered the best method of being accepted.

Each time the scanning camera was pointing away, it practised eye-opening, tiny arm movements and improved its dexterity with the fingers and toes.

Now it opened the mouth and made a noise. That wasn't good. It tried again. 'Ayefloky.' Not good enough. Practice. Practice would make perfect. The Roy thing knew what it was doing and tried to prevent it, to no avail. Its control was almost total now and Roy's consciousness was imprisoned deep within.

'Aye fol kay, ay filo kay.' It needed a shorter sound. 'Ay, ey, I.' That was better. 'Fill, fiyl, fel, fiel, feel.' Yes, better. 'ey kay, ay kay, okay.' Much nearer.

Now concentrate on the tongue, the shape of the lips, the breathing. 'I feel okie, I feel okah, I feel okay.' Yes, but much work to do. It needed to be around people. This isolation didn't help.

Its practice went on for hours.

22 More Tests

When I awoke, Linda was draped across me. The one-sixth gravity meant her body and leg were light as feathers yet provided all the expected sensual warmth and softness. I lay still, enjoying the intimacy, not wishing to wake her. I thought about the previous day.

I wondered if what had attacked Roy really could be some sort of parasite. There had certainly been something on the wheel rim. From what little we saw of it in the video sequence, it seemed to pulse neon blue, two or three times. That would explain why Roy stopped vacuuming and bent down to examine it. What had it done to him? Roy was a really strong character. I had been sure he was headed for great things. I thought he might be the next commander when Blake returned to Earth the week after next.

Before long, my caressing of her leg caused Linda to stir. She pushed her blonde hair from her eyes and kissed my cheek.

'Morning,' I said.

'Mmmh,' she replied.

Last night she had been terribly upset about whatever had infected Roy. I tried to emphasise that it might just be a drug he'd inhaled, even though I was already assuming it was a parasite. It was most unlike Linda to panic. We'd discovered our mutual fondness during basic astronaut training, a couple of years previously. She'd always been the cool, calm and collected one in emergencies and had never once shown signs of panic. Worry, yes, but she was always able to get outside the problem to come up with a solution.

On one occasion, during a simulated landing, I lost control of the simulator and thought it would crash. I remember resigning myself to the inevitable *You are dead* alert, but Linda grabbed the controls from me and fought tooth and nail to regain stability and achieved a passable, if somewhat bouncy landing. She treated every challenge as life or death, and hated being defeated, whether it be in space or on the chess board.

When she discovered the table tennis equipment in the Moonbase recdome, she became an absolute demon. It was so peculiar to play on the moon. Balls moved fast enough when you hit them hard, but trajectories, lobs and spin shots were totally different up here. No one in the base could beat her.

I couldn't believe that the nervous, shaking woman who crawled into my bed last night was the same person. She threw herself into her lovemaking as if escaping from the world. Absolutely exhausting! Then she collapsed into the deepest of sleeps.

'You a bit better?' I said.

'Think so, but I have an ominous and discomforting feeling about what's happened to Roy. I'd rather not be alone for a while.'

'I won't throw you out.'

'What time is it?'

'Time to get up. Seven.'

'Would you like ten more minutes, maybe?' she asked, looking deep into my eyes.

She was irresistible. 'Sounds good,' I said, and tenderly pulled her face to mine.

- o O o -

In the common room, we always tried to breakfast together to discuss plans for the day. We sat around the breakfast bar. Crystal was on a twelve-hour stint in the Comdome, so there were only the six of us today. Roy's sense of humour seemed a strange absence.

'Any change?' I asked as Tosh sat down with some cereal and toast.

'Well, strange again. You remember how Roy's BP and pulse were being controlled? Well, it's no longer happening. This morning, I tried several times to huff and puff about pulse and BP readings and it had absolutely no effect whatsoever.'

'That's good, isn't it? Means he's returning to normal,' said Jenny.

'I suppose so, but having seen the video again, I really don't like it at all. Linda asked me if he was possessed yesterday… Everything I've seen so far supports that.'

'I meant by a spirit,' said Linda.

'Yes, I know you did. But what if that blue thing on the rim of the wheel was a virus or creature that has possessed him somehow?'

'I went back into the garage last night,' said Blake, 'and carried out a detailed search of the wheel in question.'

'Hope you were wearing a suit,' said Mary.

'Too damned right I was.'

'And you found nothing?' asked Jenny.

'Nothing at all, and no sign of anywhere that anything could have been hiding.'

'Between the tyre and rim?' I asked.

'I suppose so, but given its size in the video, it would have needed to have compressed itself to the nth degree to get through that gap.'

'John. The patient's head is moving,' said the computer.

We were all on our feet in a flash and dashing to the lightweight airtight suits. Tosh, Jenny and I reached the surgery first.

'Jenny. Can you wait for the others and keep the door shut? Mark, come with me. When the others get here, call us on the intercom and I'll let you in if I can. Ready, Mark?'

I nodded.

'Computer, unlock the ward door.'

'Ward door unlocked, John.'

Tosh turned the handle and the door opened inwards. First, he looked around the partially open door, then stepped into the room with me in tow.

'Shut the door, Jenny.'

'Blake's here, Tosh,' she said.

'Okay, let Blake in and then close the door.'

Roy appeared to be awake. He had folded his pillow to prop his head up.

'Someone is around then?' Roy said, slowly and somewhat slurred.

'Let me have a look at you, Roy,' said Tosh. First he examined the computer monitor, then he checked Roy's pulse manually, took his temperature and shone a light into his eyes. 'How do you feel?'

'I feel okay,' said Roy.

'No pain anywhere?'

'No, no pain anywhere. Fuzzy head though.'

'Whereabouts?'

'Front, left side,' he said, lifting his hand to his forehead. 'In here.'

'Okay. I'll give you something for that. Do you know what happened to you?'

'No. I just started shaking.'

'Did you see or touch anything on the buggy?'

'Do not think so.'

'Do you remember driving out to Onizuka Hill?'

'What? Why would I do that?'

'He sounds weird,' I whispered to Blake. His voice seemed slow, slurred and his diction stilted.

'Well, he's been in a sort of coma,' said Blake.

'You drove a buggy out to Onizuka Hill, and Mark and I had to come and get you.'

'Really? Is Mark okay?'

'You know who Mark is, then?'

'Yes. Why shouldn't I?'

'You've been out for two days.'

'Really. Did not know.'

'Tosh, the rest of us are here,' said Jenny on the radio.

'Not just now, Jenny. Out,' said Tosh on the radio. Then, to Roy, 'Where do you live?'

'My family live in... Concord, New Hampshire, but I go wherever... NASA wants me to go. I live here right now.'

'So odd, that slow speech,' I whispered.

'Yes. See what you mean,' said Blake.

'Okay, Roy. I want you to rest. I'll be back in about twenty minutes to give you one or two tests, then maybe you can get out of bed.'

'Sounds good, John.'

'There's water on the cupboard.'

'Thank you. Is Mark about?'

'He's standing over there by the door with Blake. He'll come back with me later,' said Tosh.

Roy lifted his head to look at me and waved his free hand. I waved back. 'See you later, mate,' I said.

Tosh joined us and we entered the main surgery together.

'Well?' said Jenny.

'He seems okay. Speech a little slurred, but all critical readings fine. I don't think we should all descend upon him right now. I'll get Mark to help me with the scan later and after that you can come and visit in pairs.'

'Don't like that slow, deliberate speech, Tosh,' I said.

'No, and did you notice he called me John?'

'Yes. Only the computer calls you John,' said Blake.

'Something's not right. Anyway, I'm going to finish my breakfast. Out of my surgery, the lot of you,' he said, and we all made our way out. 'Computer, lock the ward door.'

'Locking the ward door, John.'

Tosh and I kept our suits on but the others went to change.

When we were all together again in the common room, Blake announced that he was cancelling all exterior work today.

'Tell Crystal, will you, Jenny?' he added.

'No problem,' said Linda. 'I've some work to do in the atmosdome. Will you work with me, Mary? I'm still a bit spooked from yesterday.'

Mary smiled and nodded.

'Did Roy seem okay to you?' Linda asked me.

'Frankly, no,' I replied. 'I'll let you know what I think after the scan.'

After breakfast Linda and Mary went to the atmosdome, Jenny to the biodome via the comdome, and Blake set to work rescheduling the rosters for our diminished numbers and planning a long report call to NASA.

Tosh and I went to the surgery to prepare for the scan.

Roy lay in bed in his strange condition, waiting for us to return.

23 Could Do Better

That was not totally successful. Must put more expression into the speech. It sensed the others were not convinced. It must do better if it was to be accepted.

Why did the doctor take on a strange expression when it mentioned his name? It dug into the memories of Roy. Once again, the creature had hidden information. Yes, John was the man's name, but no one called him John except the Moonbase computer. All the humans called him Tosh.

It enveloped what was left of Roy's consciousness with pain, like thousands of needles sticking in the skin. Round and around and around the pain went, tormenting the mind which had now retreated into the farthest reaches of the brain. It sensed Roy's internal screams and stopped the agony, warning him not to repeat the attempt to reveal its true nature.

It needed a reason for Roy's strange speech and behaviour. It needed a *story* to explain the slow speech.

'Arghh!' it cried out and flicked its hand, pulling it from the bedclothes and shaking it until the camera pointed away, then falling back onto the bed, breathing deeply, gasping and finally resting.

The story was in place.

Now, this scan. What would it be? What sort of scan? Roy wasn't familiar with the process. It stopped the application of pain when it became obvious the human mind didn't know any more. Instead, it delved deep into the lost knowledge sections of the brain for all the facts, once heard, but never consciously retained.

Computed tomography! What was that? Ah, yes, X-ray slices! Could X-rays be damaging? Yes, but more damaging to the body than to it. So that was okay. No need to hide from the scan but it must make itself appear to be a normal part of the brain. Where to go during the scan? It recalled that part of Roy which seemed familiar when it first took control. Yes. It writhed within his brain, drew itself into a long strand and made its way to safety, wrapped so tightly around the left hippocampus that it would appear as nothing more nor less than blood vessels.

It heard the door unlock and propped up Roy's head to see the Tosh creature and the friend, Mark. It had studied Mark and Roy's relationship memories. Could it convince the friend that Roy was back to normal? It needed access to the remaining astronauts and it couldn't get that if it were imprisoned here. It stabbed Roy with pain for causing it difficulties and making it hard to behave normally.

Roy's silent scream echoed around the skull.

24 Scan

As we left the common room, the computer said, *'John, a noise and sudden movements in the ward.'*

'Quick,' Tosh said, and we pulled on our helmets and started the air supply.

As we entered the surgery Tosh ordered the computer to unlock the ward door and within seconds we were inside. All seemed quiet. Roy lifted his head and said, 'About bloody time. I'm famished. How do I get some food?'

He sounded so much better and more natural.

'You okay?' I asked.

'Much better. What happened to me? Woke a few seconds ago and suddenly starving.'

'That's fine, Roy. We'll do the CT scan and then get you a meal.'

'Could do with it being the other way around, Tosh.'

'Ha. It'll only take a few minutes. Patients should be patient!' replied Tosh.

I noted Roy's use of Tosh instead of John, and was sure Tosh had too.

'Do you remember our visit earlier?' Tosh asked.

'What visit?'

'I told you about your trip out in the buggy and having to rescue you.'

'Eh? What are you on about? What trip?'

'You drove out in the buggy and then conked out and we had to use the tunnel to get to you.'

'No. Seriously?'

'What do you remember from earlier?' I asked.

'Nothing. I just woke up.'

'Let's do the scan, Mark, and then we can get some food for Roy.'

'Yes. Let's get on with it,' said Roy. 'Why're you guys in airtight suits?'

'Just a precaution in case you'd picked up a cold or something,' said Tosh.

Roy looked at us as if we were crazy.

Tosh disconnected the drip and ECG terminals and we wheeled Roy into the surgery.

'Computer, reduce pressure in the surgery by two percent.'

'Reducing pressure by two percent, John.'

I guessed Tosh wanted the pressure to be negative to draw air from outside while Roy was in the room – or rather, to not allow air out into the rest of Moonbase.

'Lie limply, Roy. Mark's going to help me get you onto the scanner.'

'I can get on myself,' said Roy and began to rise.

Tosh pushed him back down with a firm hand in the chest. 'Not until I say so, Roy.'

'Okay, Tosh.'

We lifted him bodily onto the platform and then slid him into the scanner.

'Lie absolutely still, Roy,' said Tosh.

We withdrew behind a lead shield and the scanner started. As it was only scanning Roy's head, the process took about three minutes.

We lifted him off the scanner, back onto the bed and pushed it back to the ward.

'What would you like for breakfast?' asked Tosh.

'Three eggs, bacon, hash browns, pancakes, maple syrup and some toast. Oh, and some coffee.'

I laughed. That was exactly the sort of thing the old Roy would say. Was he really back to normal?

'So, that's a bowl of cereal and fruit and a slice of toast,' I said.

He grinned at me. The old, cheeky Roy.

'Okay. Mark can get that for you while I look at the scans,' said Tosh.

We left the room. 'Computer, lock the ward door.'

'Locking the ward door, John.'

'He seems back to normal,' I said.

'Yes. A real change and he remembers nothing prior to us returning to the room. The earlier conversation is completely forgotten.'

'Do you think whatever it was has left him?'

'Don't know. Scan results first. You get his breakfast.'

-oOo-

I left Roy eating his light breakfast and joined Tosh in the surgery. He and Blake were poring over the scan.

'So, nothing?' said Blake.

'No, but if it *is* a parasite, I wonder if it might conceal itself elsewhere in the body. We ought to do a full body scan,' said Tosh.

'Did you check the video, Tosh?'

'Good point. The computer said there were sudden movements prior to us entering the ward earlier. Let's take a look.'

We hurried over to the computer terminal.

'Computer, what time did we enter the ward after breakfast?' asked Tosh.

'Nine fifty-three, John.'

'Computer, run the video of the ward from nine fifty.'

'Running that video, John.'

Roy was moving about under the sheet.

'Computer, rewind two minutes.'

'Rewinding two minutes, John.'

Now Roy was lying quietly.

'Damn nuisance that the camera scans from side to side. He's out of shot about ten percent of the time,' I said.

The video was passing right to left, and with Roy only just in view we saw him sit bolt upright and shout out as if in pain.

As the camera came back, we could clearly see him shaking his left hand as if a giant spider were on it. We missed the end of the sequence and when the camera swung back, Roy was lying still, as if asleep.

We continued watching. He raised his head, yawned and looked towards the door as we entered.

'Damnit! Did he shake it off? Is it somewhere in the ward now?' asked Tosh.

'What, the entity he picked up off the buggy wheel?' asked Blake.

'Yes,' I said. 'We might have contaminated Moonbase.'

'Computer, has any object left the ward other than human?'

'Many things, John. I can provide a list, but it is extensive.'

'Computer, were any of the items animate?'

'Yes. You and Mark left with Roy. You all returned. You and Mark came out together. Mark went back in with food and then returned here. No other animate object passed through the doorway.'

'Computer, what animate objects are currently in the ward?'

'Only Roy, John.'

'Computer, please confirm that there is nothing small, unidentified, but alive.'

'Nothing small, unidentified and alive, John.'

'What do you think?' asked Blake.

'I think that whatever it was, he managed to throw it off,' said Tosh.

'Then where is it?' I asked.

'Yes. Puzzling. He certainly seems to have returned to normal,' said Tosh.

I agreed.

'What do we do? I'll do another examination of him, but I can't see anything wrong. He might as well rejoin the rest of us.'

'I don't know,' I said. 'We ought to find that blue entity first.'

'The computer says there's nothing in there except Roy,' said Tosh.

'Do your examination, Tosh, but don't release him yet. I'll be back in a minute,' said Blake. He studied the door and its surrounds before he opened it and left the surgery.

I sat at the computer terminal to watch the video again. Tosh returned to the ward to begin a thorough physical examination of Roy.

Blake returned. 'Where's Tosh?'

'With Roy.'

77

'We were going to remain in pairs when with him?'

'Never thought. Do you think there could still be a problem? I was on my own when I served him his breakfast.'

'Oh. I think we should have remained in pairs,' said Blake.

We both looked at the ward door and dashed in.

Phew. No problem. Tosh was checking Roy's reflexes.

He looked around. 'What's up with you guys?'

'Just concerned you're on your own,' said Blake.

'Nah. He's got me with him,' said Roy.

Blake laughed.

'Why have you stripped off your airtight gloves, Tosh?' I said.

'Have you tried examining a patient with your fingers in one of those suits? Not possible. Anyway, he's completely recovered,' said Tosh.

'You sure?' asked Blake.

'Positive. He's fit as a fiddle.'

25 Double Trouble

Mark and the doctor seemed to have accepted that a change had come over Roy, and that he had recovered. Keeping Roy constrained was the key. It was able to control not just motor functions, but also the sound and emphasis of its speech. Hearing the others in conversation was helpful. Delving deeply into Roy's mind, without his interference, provided important clues to the behaviour it must adopt to be seen as "back to normal". It made a conscious decision not to say anything which it had not personally checked within Roy's memories. No more was it going to be misled by Roy's attempt to warn the others, calling Tosh 'John' and other deliberate ploys.

It was pleased with itself at its introduction of humour and Roy's characteristic cheekiness into the banter during the scan and then the breakfast conversation.

The doctor entered the room and began a full medical examination, but it was clear the airtight suit was a problem for him. He cursed several times. Eventually he removed the glove sections so that he could better feel the muscles, sinews and bones of his patient. Airtight suits were far less sensitive than the latex gloves he pulled on. What good fortune – the latex was no barrier to it.

Careful now. There must not be noise. It rubbed Roy's face with one hand and kept the right arm clear of the covering sheet. It divided. One section remained in Roy's brain; the second slithered through flesh and sinew into the thorax, as central as possible, waiting for the right moment.

The doctor's hands pressed into Roy's abdomen. It acted. In an instant, it was through Roy's skin, through the slight resistance of the latex and into the doctor.

The doctor realised. He tried to shout out, but, with its new knowledge of the human body, the shout never got beyond the intake of breath. The body fell, but Roy's arm was ready, grasping the doctor's bicep and preventing a noisy collapse to the floor.

Two seconds later it was in control. Clumsily, Tosh stood. It manipulated muscles to experiment with fingers, legs and arms. The process was over within a minute.

Internally, Tosh was fighting back. He realised what had happened and resisted every attempt to move his body and limbs, but pain soon dulled the response. It surrounded and squeezed Tosh's consciousness into a tiny corner of the brain where the human's essence could be kept temporarily until it had time to constrain it properly. Quick, quick, quick! It was done. The mind was stilled, its control rapidly approaching perfection. All it had learned from Roy, it put to use inside Tosh.

The friend and the Moonbase commander hurried into the room, though far too late to see anything out of the ordinary.

It had doubled its number. Six more humans remained. First it needed to recover and strengthen both of its components.

Time. It needed time.

26 Quarantine

'Tosh, reseal your airtight suit, right now!' said Blake forcefully.

'It's not necessary, Blake. He's fully recovered,' protested Tosh.

'The last time I checked, I was commander. You *will* reseal your suit immediately.'

Tosh reluctantly removed the latex gloves, resealed his arms with the airtight suit gloves, then closed his visor.

'Is this really necessary?' asked Roy.

'Yes,' Blake said, 'and we're putting this entire lab in quarantine. Did I feel a pressure drop when I came into the surgery?'

'Yes. I'm not stupid, you know. The medical section is at 98 percent,' said Tosh.

'Well, seeing you with your faceplate open and gloves off, I'm not so sure about whether or not you're stupid! Anyway, the entire surgery is now in quarantine. Set up low pressure for the surgery and slightly lower still for the wards and cold store.'

'We don't have an airlock on the surgery, Blake,' said Tosh.

'I'm not really so bothered about airborne bugs, Tosh, but it's still necessary. That thing had real size to it. At least the size of a finger, so until we find it, we'll always be in pairs when we come in here, and each person must check the other for anything hidden on the suits before leaving the surgery.'

'Blake! That's over the top,' Tosh said.

'Well, I don't think it is! You were downright irresponsible when you examined him – not only with airtight gloves compromised, but alone too. I don't know what you were thinking of! Thank goodness nothing happened, but we're not going to make any further blunders. I want the entity found. Alive or dead, it must be in here somewhere.'

'What about me?' asked Roy. 'I don't want to be left alone if it's still in here.'

'Sorry, Roy. You're stuck in the surgery until this entity is found. Mark, Tosh, set up ward two for Roy. Full check of everything you take from here to there. Preferably, make that nothing.'

'Ha. You want me to walk nude to ward two?' said Roy scornfully.

'That's a damn good idea, Roy. Tosh, Mark, make it so. Computer, Roy's passwords to be denied.'

'You're kidding,' said Roy.

'I'm not,' said Blake.

'Denying all of Roy's passwords, Blake.'

'Come on, Blake,' said Roy. 'That's a bit draconian. You're imprisoning me!'

'Tosh, Mark, set it up. No arguments, Roy. When it's done, I want a full meeting in the comdome. Computer, passwords required to enter or exit the surgery and ward two.'

'Establishing "passwords required" system to enter or exit the surgery and to enter or exit ward two, Blake,' confirmed the computer.

Blake turned away and left the surgery.

'That was pretty silly, breaking quarantine for your examination, Tosh,' I said.

'I know. Didn't think. I thought Roy was okay. Will you help me set up ward two, Mark?'

'No problem.'

'I can't believe this,' said Roy.

'Sorry, mate. It does make sense,' I said.

We locked ward one and spent the next forty minutes setting up ward two to be slightly homelier, with a couple of easy chairs, movie and audio player, plus a refrigerator containing a few drinks and snacks. Once that was done, we made Roy strip and stand with his arms raised as we walked around him to check the entity wasn't hanging on to him. He then walked through to take up residency in ward two.

'I'll come and sit with you later, Roy,' I said, before locking him in.

Tosh and I examined each other for anything unusual and left the surgery for some food and then the meeting in the comdome.

- o O o -

The comdome wasn't as conducive for a meeting as the common room, but given that one member of the crew always had to be on com duty, it was the only place in which we could hold a meeting of the full crew. However, there was no need for Crystal to sit at the com desk, so all seven of us sat in a circle.

'Right, everyone,' began Blake, 'Roy is under quarantine as of now. Somehow, the entity that we saw on the rim of the wheel seems to have been thrown off by him and it looks as if he's fully recovered. Mark knows him pretty well and can't see anything untoward about him.'

'I didn't say that, Blake,' I said. 'There's still an odd look in his eyes. I've known him years. Probably no one else would notice it. Just something I'm uneasy about.'

'Yes, but that's why he's in quarantine. People can visit him only in pairs. I don't care if it's a short visit, such as taking a book to him. No one, under any circumstances, must visit him on their own.'

'On the record, I don't think it's necessary and *I'm* the doctor!' said Tosh.

'That's noted, Tosh, but I make the rules. Every time you go in to see him you must be accompanied. Understand?'

Tosh nodded.

'Does that mean the danger to the rest of us has passed?' asked Linda.

'Yes. As long as we don't break quarantine. We're also as certain as we can be that the entity, whatever it was, is in ward one. I'm going to take advice from NASA about fumigating it. I've had the computer put the lock on the door to ward one on double security. It'll need two of us to be at the door before it will obey an order to unlock it.'

'But not ward two?' asked Mary.

'No.'

'It would ensure none of us could visit him alone,' she said.

'I suppose so. Yes. Computer, put ward two on double security.'

'Putting ward two on double security, Blake.'

'Is that really necessary?' asked Tosh, throwing his arms up. 'It really is a bit over the top, frankly.'

'Sorry, Tosh. I disagree. Also, airtight suits must be worn to visit Roy and we are maintaining the surgery on 98 percent pressure and wards one and two and the cold store under 96 percent pressure.'

'What? You think there could be bugs in there as well?' asked Linda.

'No, not really, but quarantine is quarantine. Now, all of you, back to your normal duties. Tosh will put out a general call on the intercom radios if he needs someone to visit Roy with him. Mary and Jenny, go and visit him, pick up his spirits, find out what he'd like to eat and cook him a really nice lunch. After all, this isn't poor Roy's fault. Meeting over. Computer, minutes to each of us and NASA.'

'Preparing minutes, distributing to each of the crew and to NASA, Blake.'

27 Recovery

It was separated now from its other half, but both parts knew the plan. Soon they would be able to converse with each other. Just one more human host would allow them to overcome the security measures put in place by the Moonbase commander.

In the meantime, it knew both its components were physically exhausted. The division had not been an easy process. Both were weakened. Now they must recover their strength. The Tosh component was working on minimal energy, trying to rest the body while its tendrils explored the fascinating knowledge acquired during the doctor's forty-five years of life.

It learned more about the orbiting platform which circled the moon every sixty minutes. Currently there were two beings on board, but four more were on their way from Earth. Those weren't due to come to Moonbase, but to the Chinese habitat a few tens of kilometres away.

Both components understood that their objective was to get one of them to the nearby planet. A single infected person moving freely on Earth and the planet would belong to it.

Every two to three days it would be able to divide. One, two, four, eight, 16, 32, 64, then 128 in less than a month. After that point the escalation would be extraordinary. 256, 512, 1024, 2048, 4096, 8192, 16,000, 32,000, 64,000, 128,000 after two months. 128 million in three, 128 billion in four. The world would be its domain.

Getting one of its components to Earth was the objective. Blake and Jenny were due to return to Earth in a fortnight. Patience, recovery and taking control.

But some of the humans were still suspicious – particularly the friend of Roy and the female, Linda, although her concern seemed mainly intuition.

It had what Roy's mind told it was a eureka moment. It *knew* how to defuse suspicion.

28 Visiting Hours

Linda, Mary and I had a light lunch together of bread, salad, ham and pickles. We ate from plastic boxes as we sat in the biodome. I was a relative newcomer to Moonbase, but enjoying the shrubs and greenery was increasingly important to me. They grew prolifically in the controlled environment. I loved the relaxing sound of clucking hens which came from their coop at the far end of aisle one. If I was alone, I'd happily while away my breaks watching them scratching in their litter. Bees buzzed by quite often too. They'd been newly introduced and seemed to be doing well. The dome was kept at 22 degrees centigrade and the humidity was higher than the rest of Moonbase for obvious reasons. Part of the dome was shaded with blinds as we were in the middle of the lunar day and, while it might be cold and airless outside, in here the heat of the sun could kill the plants swiftly if they weren't protected.

'Do you think he's okay now?' asked Mary.

'I don't,' said Linda.

'Why? Blake and I visited him this morning and he seemed back to his old self.'

'Don't know. Just something spooks me when I'm with him.'

'What about you, Mark? You know him better than any of us,' Mary said.

'Everything seems back to normal, even his sense of humour, but I'm not convinced. There's something about his eyes.'

'What do you mean?'

'They're sort of glazed over. I noticed it when we'd got him into ward two and I was sitting on his bed, chatting.'

'Glazed?' said Mary. 'Didn't notice anything like that.'

'Linda and I are going to see him after lunch. I'll take a hard look at him, but while the rest of us smile and even talk with our eyes, his just seem to hold the same stare, as if he's not really listening or seeing us.'

'I'll look next time I go. He does blink, doesn't he?'

'Oh yes, he blinks,' I said.

'What is it that bothers you, Linda?'

'Can't put my finger on it,' replied Linda. 'I just feel uncomfortable with him. Difficult to explain, really. I baked some more of those brownies. Last week he was gushing about how much he liked them. I'd like to see how he reacts this time.'

'Let me know. I've got to get back to the geodome,' said Mary, picking up her lunch box and heading to the exit. She shouted back, 'And save me a brownie!'

Linda and I used our temporary isolation to enjoy a kiss.

'I do love it that we're seeing each other again,' I said.

'Should I move in?' she asked.

'Please.'

'You won't let me down this time?'

We'd moved in together during astronaut training, but I'd done a silly thing. Another girl batted her eyes at me and, foolishly, I didn't say no. Linda was justifiably furious. She wouldn't answer my calls and three days later I moved to Cape Canaveral. We didn't see each other again until I arrived here a couple of weeks ago. We'd never talked about what happened. We'd spent the odd night together here, but very informally. The moon's gravity was an incredible aphrodisiac… the things you could do were quite amazing!

'I promise. I was stupid and thoughtless.'

We kissed again, she caressed my cheek, and we headed back to the common room to get the brownies for Roy.

- o O o -

Tosh wasn't in the surgery. We checked the notes on the door to ward two, but there were no special instructions. We both entered our passwords, then I cracked open the door and knocked on it.

'Yes. Come in,' called Roy.

Ward two was about five metres across with one wall following the curve of the dome. A window provided a view of the tunnel that led to the biodome and a small section of the dome itself.

Roy had been sitting in one of the easy chairs, but he stood up as we entered.

'I brought you some of my cakes,' Linda said, passing a plastic container to Roy.

'Ooh, thanks, Linda.' He removed the lid. 'They look good. Can I share?'

'Thought you'd never ask, but it's difficult to eat in these suits!' I said and laughed.

'Anything you need?' asked Linda.

'Yes. I'd like to get out of here. It's so boring. Just watched that new Greg Ellis film, *Purpled*. Frankly, not a great piece of cinema.'

'The critics are saying that, but I thought it was okay,' I said.

'Ah, but you like anything with petite blondes in it. No wonder you two hooked up again!'

'Shut up, Roy, or no more cakes,' said Linda.

We talked for about forty minutes. I watched him the entire time, and listened to his speech carefully in case anything didn't ring true.

'Right, we'll leave you the rest of the brownies and get back to work,' I said.

We stood up, as did Roy. I slapped him on the back and gave him a brief man-hug, while Linda ran her hand down from the back of his head to his shoulder.

'You need a shave,' she said.

'I know.'

I unlocked the door and got a shock when I opened it. Tosh was standing outside, looking straight at us.

'You gave me a fright, Tosh,' said Linda.

'Oh, hi you two. Sorry, Linda. I must check his readings,' he said.

'I'll wait with you,' I said. 'You go on, Linda. See you later.'

'Right,' she said.

'No need to stay, if you want to get on,' Tosh said. 'It'll only take a minute.'

'It's all right, Tosh. I'll wait. No point in rules if we're going to break them. Hadn't you better close your face mask?'

'Oh, yes,' he said, sealing his suit.

Tosh spent a few minutes checking blood pressure and temperature, then joined me at the door. I pulled it shut behind us. The red light illuminated to show that it was locked.

'Oh, I left my pen,' Tosh said.

We both entered our passwords, me ensuring the keypad was covered. Then Tosh slapped his white coat pocket. 'Oh no, here it is,' he said, taking out the pen.

'Computer, lock ward two door,' I said.

'Locking ward two door, Mark.'

'I'll see you later, Tosh,' I said, and left the surgery, turning right along the main corridor. I'd some work to do in the garage this afternoon, including changing the wheel on buggy three. Had Tosh tried to con me into leaving the door unlocked after I'd used my password a second time? Odd, that business with the pen.

- o O o -

'I saw what you meant,' Linda said, curling herself around behind me.

'The eyes?'

'Yes. I've seen the same thing on a hypnosis subject at college.'

'Sort of vacant, isn't it?'

'Yes, but what does it mean?'

I turned to face her and pulled her towards me. 'I don't know, Linda. I wish we could find that entity in ward one. If we definitely knew we had it, then I might feel easier about Roy.'

'He liked my brownies. Wasn't quite as excited about them this time, but not in a spooky way. I s'pose new cakes aren't as exciting the second time. He said he'd never had homemade brownies before.'

'But you saw what I meant about the eyes? I'm not getting paranoid, then?' I asked.

'No, it's real enough but it's the odd feeling I get in his company which affects me most. Never had that before.'

'Did you hear what Blake said about quarantine?'

'No, what?'

'He thinks it might cause his and Jenny's departure to be delayed.'

'No.'

'Yes. NASA's a bit spooked by the whole event. They want us to find the entity before they'll allow the flight.'

'How do we do that?' she asked.

'Blake says he's building a detector.'

'It's alien life, Mark. We keep forgetting the importance of what's happened in the scheme of things.'

'Yes. I should feel excited, but instead, I'm apprehensive. How could Roy forget driving out to Onizuka Hill and then forget the conversation from earlier in the day when he regained consciousness?'

'Seems wrong, doesn't it? Could it be intelligent?'

'Maybe, Linda. It seems impossible for something so small to harbour intelligence, but if it *is* intelligent, it would explain a lot.'

'First an attempt to run away, then, realising that wasn't a good plan, it allowed us to bring it back. Almost as if it's learning about us.'

'I don't like it, Linda.'

'You see what I mean, then? It's creepy. Is Roy lying there, waiting to get out and kill us all?'

'Don't know. I suppose it could be controlling him, but Roy would find a way of letting us know.'

'How?' she asked.

'Maybe he already did, by calling Tosh 'John',' I said.

'Yes. That was really weird. I wouldn't even know Tosh's name if it wasn't for the computer. But he was back to normal shortly afterwards.'

'Maybe it realised that Roy was giving clues to us and shut down the opportunity. I asked him several things that only he and I would know and there wasn't a problem with any of his answers,' I said.

'Could it be dipping into his memories?' Linda said. 'God, it's horrific to think about something living inside you, controlling your thoughts and movements.'

'Let's keep our eyes open. It'd be good to find the entity and know that it's resolved once and for all.'

'I don't think there *is* anything to find,' said Linda. 'I don't think anything came out of him. We didn't actually see it, did we? It happened while the camera wasn't on him. It could have been staged for our benefit.'

'Right, I see what you mean, but that would mean the entity understands our thought processes extremely well.'

'I think he's still infected.'

'Let's stick together,' I said.

'Now *that's* the best idea you've had for at least thirty minutes!' she said, and pulled me closer.

29 Planning

It had now tried three times to get access to the Roy component on its own. First it had been foiled by Crystal and Jenny, then by Mary, and the latest was Mark, who wouldn't compromise the safety systems. It had Mary alone, but neither it nor Roy's version had been able to divide. They needed another day.

However, now it had a plan to defuse suspicion, it hoped it would be able to make a case to release Roy from quarantine. To do that it must get in to see Roy alone.

The perfect opportunity might come in the morning, soon after breakfast.

30 A New Day

'Top up?'

'Thanks, Linda,' I said as she took my cup.

We were all eating breakfast in the common room, other than Roy, who was still in isolation, and Mary, who was on com duty.

'And you think this gadget will find the entity that attacked Roy?' asked Crystal.

'Well, it's based on an infrared detector, but NASA have given me a list of instructions to enhance it,' said Blake, holding up the schematic he'd been reading. 'If the entity has even the slightest temperature above ambient, it should show up. I'm going to get the computer to drop the ward one temperature suddenly, prior to the scan.'

'Sounds as if it should work,' said Tosh. 'Are we ready to release Roy yet?'

'No. NASA is being firm on this. We must find the entity before they'll sanction lifting quarantine,' said Blake.

'Mark said that your return flight might be postponed, Blake,' said Linda.

'Yes, possibly.'

I heard Jenny whisper, 'Oh, good,' to Crystal, who laughed.

'When do you think you'll have it ready?' I asked.

'This afternoon, with a fair wind. It's tricky circuitry, not really made to be adapted, frankly. But I'll get it done.'

'By the way, Jenny,' said Tosh, 'don't forget it's your fortnightly medical at 9.30.'

'Yes. I'll be there,' she answered.

'Come a bit earlier and bring some breakfast for Roy. He's got a toaster and coffee in the ward but could probably do with something a bit more substantial.'

'I'll poach him some eggs.'

'Are the hens laying again?' asked Linda.

'Two in the last two days. They're gradually coming back into lay,' replied Jenny. She was responsible for the hendome, as we jokingly called the biodome when the hens were being discussed.

'I miss them when they're not laying,' Crystal said.

Eggs didn't travel too well in space, but hens did. A special dome was planned to give them a more natural environment and other livestock would join them soon. Ducks and rabbits mainly, but a pool for trout and carp was also on the agenda. We'd had lettuce and some other vegetables from a cultivated section of the Biodome, but other than that, our diet of freeze-dried packet food got to be boring after a few weeks.

The components for the Livestock Dome were expected on a separate automatic supply vessel in three months' time.

Breakfast over, we all headed off to our various duties.

- o O o -

I had a busy morning preparing lists of supplies needed for the garage. We had two new crew members due to join us when Blake and Jenny left, and they would bring what I ordered, so it was a serious business. On the moon, we couldn't just pop down to the local hardware store if we didn't have a particular nut or bolt. We had a good machine shop for making anything for which we didn't have spares and as far as the buggies went, we could always scavenge one if another needed a part, then replace it when the next supply arrived. I'd even managed to repair buggy three's damaged wheel.

At lunch, I found Linda conducting the same exercise in the catering cupboards.

'Finished your stocktake?' Linda asked.

'Yes. You?'

'Yes. Tosh, Jenny, do you want tea?' Linda called across to where they were seated, eating sandwiches.

'No thanks,' said Tosh.

'Jenny?'

'No. No thanks,' she said.

'Just finishing the requisition,' she said to me as she made our tea. 'I've asked for a new kettle, too. This one's got a faulty automatic off switch.'

We sat together and enjoyed a ploughman's lunch. It had grown in popularity worldwide after the remake of *Tess* in 2021.

'I'm on com duty, starting 7pm,' said Linda.

'I'll come and keep you company for some of the time,' I said.

'John, there is movement in ward one,' said the computer.

All of us looked at Tosh.

'Did you set it for small movements?' asked Blake.

'Course I did,' he said angrily. He jumped up from his seat. 'We'd better get over there.'

'No!' said Blake. 'Comdome first. I want to look at the monitor.'

We all dropped what we were doing and ran through to the comdome. When we arrived, Mary, who'd also heard the computer message, had already put the ward one feed on the large screen.

'Anything?' asked Tosh.

'Can't see anything,' said Mary.

We all peered at the screen.

'There!' shouted Linda. 'There, by the wheel of the vital-signs monitor!'

Mary zoomed in and, sure enough, beside the monitor wheel was a lump of what looked like clear gelatine.

'Is it moving?' asked Blake.

'Can't see any movement,' I said.

Then, as clear as day, it began to slide across the ward floor.

'Stay here. Keep an eye on it. I'll be back in a moment,' said Blake. He rushed out of the room.

'Think I'll put on my suit,' I said.

'Yes,' agreed Tosh. 'Jenny, go and lie down. See if you can throw off that headache. I'll get you something for it later if it hasn't gone.'

'Okay,' she said and walked towards the door.

'Hey, hun,' said Crystal to Jenny. 'You okay? Didn't know you were unwell.'

'Yes,' Jenny replied, 'just a headache. I think a lie down will cure it.'

'I'll come and see you later,' said Crystal.

'Thanks,' replied Jenny and left the comdome.

A few seconds later, Blake dashed back into the room holding a steel cylinder about thirty centimetres in length. 'Has it moved?'

'Just slowly crossing the floor,' said Mary.

'Tosh. You, me and Mark – over to the surgery now!' said Blake. 'Mary, keep it in view.'

'Will do.'

The three of us, suited up, entered the surgery and stood outside the door to ward one.

'What's it doing now?' asked Blake over the personal intercom.

'Still crossing the room. Very slow,' said Mary.

Blake turned to us. 'Here's what we're going to do.'

Blake briefed us on his plan, then we unlocked the door, ready to dash in.

'Still no change in speed or direction, Mary?'

'Yes. It's now returning towards where we first saw it.'

'Ready, Mark?' asked Blake.

I showed him the sampler tool, which looked like an oversized sink-plunger.

'Right. Go, go, go!'

We burst into the room. Tosh slammed the door closed behind us.

I saw the entity on the floor, moving towards the monitor stand. I ran over and pushed the transparent sampler over it. We watched as it – whatever it was – moved around and around in circles, trapped.

'Disc, Tosh,' I said.

Tosh slid a wafer-thin metal disc under the sampler. Together, we lifted it off the floor, keeping the thing trapped within it.

'Okay, Blake, ready,' said Tosh.

'Don't let it slip,' I said.

Blake brought his metal cylinder over, put the screw-on lid aside and slid out a disc which would seal off the cylinder once something was inside.

'Ready?' he said. 'Don't lose sight of it if it gets away.'

'Ready,' I said, and Tosh nodded.

'If it gets out, don't let it touch you,' said Tosh.

Blake held the cylinder with the open end pointing upwards, then turned it so that he could see in through a window which ran the length of one side. Tosh and I manoeuvred the disc and sampler over the cylinder so that when Tosh pulled away the disc, the entity ought to drop into the cylinder.

Tosh said, 'Three, two, one, now!'

Tosh whipped the metal disc away. The sampler dropped down the millimetre or two to the cylinder and the entity fell downwards. Blake slid the seal back into the cylinder. Tosh and I backed off as Blake screwed the top back onto the cylinder. The flanges covered the seal plate, so nothing could now get in or out of the cylinder.

'You definitely got it?' I asked.

'Got it!' said Blake, peering in through the window.

Tosh and I had a good look at it.

'Looks like gelatine,' said Tosh.

'It's definitely alive,' I said. 'What could it be?'

'Some sort of parasite. Probably found Roy unpalatable, so got out,' replied Tosh.

'Possibly,' I said suspiciously.

'Well, at least we got it,' said Blake.

'Thank God,' said Tosh. 'Shall I release Roy?'

'No, Tosh. Not until NASA give the all-clear. I'll let you know when,' replied Blake.

'Where are you going to put it?' I asked.

'In the sterile safe in the biodome, until we know what NASA wants to do with it. Can't imagine they'd want it transported back to Earth.'

'No. They're more likely to send a team here to examine it,' said Tosh.

Once I was out of the airtight suit, I found Linda in the biodome and told her what had happened.

'But Roy's still not right,' she said.

'No. Well, NASA's keeping him in quarantine for the moment, anyway,' I said.

'Come on,' she said. 'You're not happy that Roy's back to normal either, are you? His eyes. He's not right, Mark.'

'But we've got the entity now, so it isn't in him anymore.'

'Not convinced. I don't like the look in his eyes. Perhaps part of it is still inside him.'

'You said you thought he hadn't thrown it off, but it now looks as if he did,' I reminded her.

'Trust me, Mark. Something is wrong with him.'

'I don't see what more we can do,' I said.

'I think we need to talk to others. Mary knows what we were talking about. Let's go and see her. She's on com duty.'

We packed up and walked to the comdome.

'Hi, you two,' Mary said as we entered. 'Well done catching the entity.'

'Can we talk to you about it?' I asked.

'Mary, what do you think?' Linda said.

'About what?'

'I'm still worried about Roy being possessed by something. His eyes aren't right,' said Linda.

'Oh, yes,' said Mary. 'What you said about his eyes being sort of vacant... I was going to tell you...'

'What? That's what we're worried about. What were you going to tell us?' I said hurriedly.

'Well, Tosh looks the same.'

'*What?*' Linda exclaimed.

'I took some papers in to him, and he seemed to look straight through me.'

'Tosh?' I said.

'Yes, and Jenny wasn't well when Crystal saw her at lunch,' said Mary.

'Oh, yes. The headache,' I said.

'But if Tosh is infected, when could it have happened?' asked Linda.

'Damn,' I said. 'He was examining Roy without a suit. Blake was furious about it, but Tosh didn't have a fit like Roy. He looked totally normal and was only out of my sight two or three minutes, if that.'

'Might be on the video,' Linda said. 'Oh God. Jenny had a medical today, didn't she? Tosh would have been alone with her.'

'Mary, pull up the ward one video for the morning Roy regained consciousness,' I said.

'Here we are,' Mary said.

The video showed Tosh entering the ward in his airtight suit, while I was in the surgery looking at the monitor video from earlier. Tosh walked up to Roy and began to examine him. He then slipped off his suit gloves and pulled on latex ones, so that he could feel Roy's abdomen.

All of a sudden, Tosh seemed to get an electric shock. He jumped and began to fall. Roy grabbed his bicep and stopped him crashing to the ground. Tosh's body jerked a little. Then, within a minute, he was back on his feet. Two minutes later he continued examining Roy as Blake and I entered.

'So, he was infected then?' said Linda.

'Yes,' I said, 'and the entity had him under control within a couple of minutes.'

'By now Jenny could be infected too,' Mary said.

'Let me see ward one's video for this morning,' I said.

We ran through the video at high speed, then saw Tosh enter the ward.

'What time was that?' I asked.

'Ten-fifteen,' said Mary.

Tosh and Jenny were standing in the ward. He stooped to place something on the floor near to the monitor. It was the entity, and Tosh wasn't wearing any protection.

'They put it there deliberately!' said Linda.

'Oh my God,' said Mary. 'There are already at least three of them… and Jenny and Crystal are a couple. We'll have to tell Crystal.'

'There must be a time delay before they can spread,' I said.

'Find the surgery video for 9.30, Mary,' said Linda.

Mary ran the video back on the surgery feed until we saw Tosh enter, Jenny following.

Tosh had her lie on the couch, then he put his fingers to her wrist. Immediately, Jenny jerked as if receiving a defibrillator shock. Tosh held her down until she became still. After a short while, Jenny rose clumsily from the couch and the two of them entered ward two. They both stood beside Roy, their hands connected as if they were all communicating by touch. Tosh put something into a flask. It looked like the entity. They then left ward two.

'The timing of that is immediately before they took the entity into ward one. There really are three of them and they were banking on us not watching this video,' I said.

'Where's Crystal?' asked Linda.

'Geodome,' replied Mary.

'Linda and I will go and see her and make sure she's not been taken over too. If Tosh, Jenny or Roy come in here, keep well away from them until we get back,' I said.

'Don't worry,' Mary replied. 'I won't let *anyone* anywhere near me.'

31 Sacrifice

Finally, it was ready to divide, and Roy's component would be ready too.

In order to complete the plan, it needed one of their components to be sacrificed for the good of the others. To collect it, both Tosh and Roy needed to be able to touch each other without suits. To achieve that Tosh needed to infect another person with his split parasite so that they could access ward two.

At last, the opportunity came. Jenny was due her fortnightly medical.

Like a lamb to the slaughter, she followed the doctor into his surgery and stretched herself out on the couch for the routine examination.

Tosh placed his fingers on her pulse and the transfer was almost instantaneous. It now knew a huge amount about the human anatomy, so within seconds, Jenny's protesting mind was overcome. It struggled with some of the differences between male and female, but only for a matter of seconds.

After a couple of minutes, although her parasite was exhausted from its division, it forced her to stand, and they used their codes to access ward two.

They each held hands, understanding and sharing each other's knowledge. Roy's parasite divided unequally. There was no point in sacrificing a whole parasite, so it created a smaller, barely viable part. It emerged from Roy's hand and entered a flask held by Tosh.

Next, they put the parasite onto the floor in ward one, reset the scanning camera controls and retreated into the surgery to recuperate. The parasite would wait until lunchtime, so that both Tosh and Jenny would be in the common room before it started moving, triggering the alarm.

It was a successful ruse and both Blake and Mark seemed to accept that it really was the parasite which had originally infected Roy.

Now they needed time to recover their strength and then divide again. The day after tomorrow, Jenny would infect

Crystal; Tosh would infect one of the other three humans, and another would be infected by Roy.

Only two more humans would stand in its way.

32 Getting Up To Speed

Crystal was in her white coat, studying a rock sample at the main bench in the geodome.

She turned as we entered. 'Oh, hello.'

'Hi, Crystal,' said Linda. 'We've got a problem.'

'Well, don't breathe on me!' she quipped.

'Crystal, it may sound a strange request, but can we ask you to stand up and face us?' I asked.

'What? Why?'

'There's a good reason. Honest,' said Linda.

Reluctantly, Crystal got to her feet and turned towards us.

'Hands in pockets, please,' I said.

'What the hell is this? No!'

'Please, Crystal. There really is a good reason and it's connected to the entity,' said Linda.

'What, the thing that was in Roy?'

'Yes,' I said.

Slowly and suspiciously, she put down a rock sample and slid her hands into the pockets of her coat.

'Stand still,' said Linda, approaching Crystal.

I was ready to slap Crystal's arms away if there was any attempt to touch Linda.

Linda stopped and peered into Crystal's eyes.

'She's fine,' she said and gave Crystal a hug.

'What's going on?' Crystal demanded.

'It's easier to show you. Come with us to the comdome,' I said.

'Can't I finish this job? It'll not take more than forty minutes or so.'

'No, Crystal. It's urgent,' said Linda.

'Hi, Blake,' I said into my personal intercom.

'Yes, Mark.'

'You alone?'

'Yes, why?'

'I didn't want to be overheard at your end.'

'Eh? What's the problem?'

'Can you meet us in the comdome? It's important. Don't tell anyone.'

'What? That's a bit odd.'

'It's about the entity. Please. As soon as you can.'

'Okay. I'll be there shortly.'

'Don't mention it to Tosh or Jenny.'

'No. I'll come directly. You're worrying me.'

- o O o -

After watching the crucial video sequences, the five of us huddled around the com desk. Mary had made an edited copy of the video, which was now winging its way to Neil Weston, head of Moonbase Operations at NASA.

'He'll call us as soon as it arrives, so that we can talk him through it,' said Mary.

Linda had an arm around Crystal, who was in some distress over the fact that Jenny had been taken over. 'I thought it was odd that she had a headache. She never has headaches. Are you sure?'

'You saw the video,' Linda said.

'Yes, but it's Jenny we're talking about. She's a really strong personality.'

'So was Roy,' I said.

'Look,' said Blake, 'this is a frighteningly dangerous situation. From what we've seen, it only needs one touch of skin-to-skin contact for this entity to transfer. It even went through Tosh's latex gloves. This really is perilous to all of us. We've lost three already! We could end up playing tag for our lives. How long will that video take to get to Neil, Mary?'

'I sent it low def, so should be there any minute. A high-def version is following it.'

'Hi Moonbase, got the file. Talk me through it,' said Neil two minutes later.

Mary explained exactly what was happening during each of the sequences, which included the original garage footage of Roy; Tosh being infected through the latex gloves; his transferral of the parasite to Jenny; both of them collecting the parasite from Roy and then staging the finding of the entity in ward one.

'Where is it now?' asked Neil.

'In the secure safe,' said Blake.

'Who has the key?' asked Neil after the annoying two-second lag which affected all communications between Earth and the moon.

'Good point,' said Blake. 'I've got all three keys.'

'Not a good idea,' said Neil. *'Mary's your deputy. Give her the second key and Mark the third. Crystal and Linda – you should always know where those keys are.'*

'Mine'll be on my keyring. Mary, where will you keep yours?' asked Blake.

'I've a case of Rotring pens in the geodome. It'll be under the foam inside the case,' she said.

'Mine will be on my keyring,' I said.

'Ensure they are recovered if Mark, Mary or Blake is infected at any time,' said Neil.

'I think we should get Tosh, Jenny and Roy into the surgery and lock them in,' said Linda.

'What about food?' I said. 'We can't starve them, and we know these entities can squeeze into the tiniest spaces – between the rim and tyre of that buggy wheel, for instance.'

'It can't get out of the safe, can it?' asked Mary.

'It might be able to get out of the safe, but not the sample flask. That's airtight. If it hadn't already been living in a vacuum, I'd have been worried about suffocating it,' said Blake.

'I've called in some security and military people. Think up a reason for why you're all in the comdome in case one of them comes in – and make it good! You don't want them to suspect that you know they're infected.'

'Locking them in. That's the answer,' said Linda.

'I think I agree,' said Crystal, 'but I'd like to see Jenny first, to be certain she's really infected.'

'They don't seem to be able to infect additional people for about forty-eight hours, so we should be safe tonight and tomorrow. Take a good look at her at breakfast,' I said.

'She might be in my room. We normally sleep together,' said Crystal.

'How can we find out?' said Linda.

'Wake up guys! The location system. Computer, specify Jenny's location,' said Mary.

'Jenny is in her room, Mary,' said the computer.

'Computer, where's John?' said Blake.

'John is in the surgery, Blake.'

'Computer, where's Roy?' asked Blake.

'Roy is in ward two, Blake.'

'Right, at least we know where they are,' Linda said.

'Computer, what's the status of ward two's door?' I asked.

'The door to ward two is locked, Mark.'

'What're you thinking?' asked Mary.

'I wondered if he'd had the audacity to leave it unlocked so that he could go back and forth to communicate with Roy,' I said.

'Yes, I see. They communicate by touch,' said Linda.

'What? How do you know that?' asked Blake.

'The holding of hands by Roy's bed when they collected the entity in the flask,' Mary replied.

'We need to stay together,' said Linda. 'If they get any of us alone, it would be easy to overpower us.'

'I'm hungry. Blake, can you stay with Mary while the three of us get a meal? Linda's on com duty at seven,' I said.

'Wait,' said Linda. 'Can I see your eyes, Blake?'

'Eh. Oh, okay,' said Blake. He let Linda and me examine his eyes.

'All clear,' I said.

'Computer,' said Blake, 'advise me, Mary, Crystal, Mark and Linda by personal intercom if John, Roy or Jenny change their locations.'

The computer confirmed the instruction.

'Computer, make that so until the instruction is changed by any two of the five who are being notified.'

'That instruction will be followed unless changed by any two of the notified five, Blake.'

'We'll be back soon,' I said.

Crystal, Linda and I left for the common room.

'I feel more secure now,' said Linda.

'Yes, but I'm still having trouble about Jenny being one of them,' said Crystal.

- o O o -

By eight, we'd all eaten and were back in the comdome, Linda now at the desk.

'Gave me a turn when I saw Tosh come into the common room,' said Mary.

'He just got himself a meal, did he?' Linda asked.

'He's still there. At least we know the computer instruction works well. We were both informed,' said Blake.

'Yes. We were ready to all dash through to you if needed,' said Crystal.

'That would've left Linda alone,' said Mary.

'No. We talked about it and decided an unmanned com desk was less important than sticking together,' I said.

'Yes. Suppose so,' said Blake, despite the golden rule of someone always being on com duty.

'Information. John has returned to the surgery,' said the computer.

A few seconds later, my intercom went. *'Tosh here, Mark. Can you come through so I can take food into Roy, please?'*

'Give me a minute,' I replied. 'I should be safe. I'll put my suit on here.' I climbed into it.

'I'll suit up, too, and wait in the surgery while you're in with Tosh and Roy,' said Blake.

'How do we explain that?' I said.

'Needs two of us to unlock the surgery,' said Blake.

'Good grief! So how did Tosh get out and back in again?' I said.

'Hadn't thought of that. Computer, what is the status of the surgery door lock?'

'Surgery door is locked, Blake.'

'Computer, what security is on it?'

'It can only be opened by two passwords or by John, Mary or you, Blake.'

'Computer, who changed the instruction?' asked Blake.

'The medical officer can always enter the surgery alone for safety reasons in the event of an emergency. So can the commander and deputy commander, Blake.'

'Hey, Mary. I'd forgotten that. You, me and Tosh can override some of the password-protected doors,' said Blake.

'Yes, you're right,' said Mary.

'Okay, Mark. You go in and I'll be outside in the corridor,' said Blake.

I said into the personal intercom, 'On my way, Tosh.'

'Does that work on the ward doors, Mary?' asked Linda.

'No, only the area with medical supplies, the garage, comdome and Blake's office,' she replied.

'So Tosh could get in here even if it was locked?' asked Linda.

'Yes. We ought to review all security when Mark and Blake get back. Neil will help us stay safe, I'm sure,' said Mary.

- o O o -

The delivery of Roy's food went fine, and I sat and chatted to him while he ate. I made it all as natural as possible.

Thirty minutes later he was safely locked in ward two. Tosh told me he was tired and was going to get an early night, and the five healthy crew were all back in the comdome before nine for Neil's call with military and security advisers. He'd also called in an expert on the Moonbase architecture.

'It's no good. I want to see Jenny,' said Crystal.

'She's definitely infected,' I said.

'No one has actually seen her, though. I want to check for myself. This isn't just another crew member – we're a couple. She's my partner. I'd never forgive myself if I didn't check and she *then* got infected.'

'Why don't you and Linda go?' said Blake. 'She shouldn't be dangerous yet, but don't touch her skin, just in case. It's five to nine so if you hurry now, you'll be back for the session with Neil. Literally five minutes, okay?'

'You okay with that, Linda?' I said.

'Apprehensive,' Linda said.

'I'll go if you like,' said Mary.

'No, it's okay. I'm apprehensive, but not scared. I'll go.'

'Come on then, quick,' said Crystal. They left the comdome.

I don't think any of us were positive about any of this, but we all felt better when the computer told us Tosh was in his room. We had a few hours to plan a course of action.

NASA still hadn't called when Crystal and Linda returned. I made them both stand still, hands in pockets, while I checked their eyes. There were no vacant expressions, but Crystal's eyes were full of tears. To all intents and purposes, she'd lost her partner.

'I'm so sorry, Crystal. Let's hope there's a way to put them right,' I said. She burst into another sobbing fit.

'Hello Moonbase, copy?' said Neil.

'I hate to be cruel about this, Crystal, but we need to start this session with Earth,' said Blake.

Crystal and Linda came over to the console and took seats with the rest of us, Crystal still dreadfully upset.

33 Rest And Recuperation

All three of it were resting, to recover from the dividing process. The first twenty-four hours were the most difficult. They didn't give a thought to the fourth part, which sat in hibernation inside the cylinder, locked securely within the safe. It wouldn't be hurt. Its species was evolved to lie dormant for millennia.

34 Strategy

Our video conference was productive and, ultimately, reassuring.

NASA made it very clear that there was no way an infected person could be allowed back to Earth. There was talk about sending a team of military doctors to the moon, together with neurosurgeons and various scanners which could detect the entities within the human body and thereby allow the possibility of removing them and saving the infected individuals.

We discussed a strategy to protect ourselves in the interim and to isolate the infected. This would be put in place the next morning. NASA agreed it had to be put into effect before they were strong enough to take over additional people.

Once we were safe, plans would be put in place to allow the doctors to get to Moonbase as soon as possible.

What was somewhat unnerving was that it had been made clear to us that the entire base would be destroyed rather than allow Earth to become infected.

We finished our discussions about one in the morning and then rehearsed the agreed plan so that we'd be ready to act before breakfast.

We agreed that no one would be permitted to be alone at any time until we were secure. While it was fine for Linda and me to stay together, it was not so easy for the other two women and Blake. However, Linda was on com duty until 7am anyway, so Blake and I moved collapsible beds into the comdome. Mary and Crystal went to Mary's room, which was larger than Crystal's.

Blake snored, and I didn't sleep well. I ended up sitting with Linda from about four in the morning, as we whispered our thoughts and worries to each other. Our biggest concerns were that we hadn't taken every possibility into account and that the entities could have imparted some superhuman strength into their hosts. We planned to use tasers to control them but had no idea if they'd be effective against them.

At seven, Crystal and Mary arrived. Crystal was on com duty for the next twelve hours. Now was the time to execute the plan.

Our first duty was to check each other's eyes to ensure we were still human, then we put on the lightweight airtight suits. Once we were all ready, Blake spoke into the master intercom.

'Hi, Blake here. We have a problem to resolve. All crew except Roy, please come to the comdome immediately.'

Now we waited, more than a little fearfully. Linda's hand found its way into mine as we stood with our backs to the wall, just beside the door.

Tosh marched into the room, followed a few seconds later by Jenny. They didn't see us. We moved across to the door to prevent them exiting as they took seats near to Blake and Crystal.

'What's going on? Why are you all suited up?' Tosh asked, as he looked around the room and noticed us guarding the door and Mary holding a taser.

'Cryss, what's happening?' Jenny asked Crystal.

'Sorry, Tosh, Jenny, but you're both infected with a parasite which was originally picked up by Roy,' said Blake.

'Nonsense,' said Tosh. 'You were with me when we caught it and sealed it in the sample cylinder.'

'Sorry, that was just a ploy. All of you contain one or more of these entities and we cannot allow you to infect us,' said Blake.

'Stand up,' said Mary, 'and make your way to the door, slowly. Any sudden movement and I'll taser you. Be in no doubt that I will.'

Tosh and Jenny didn't move. Tosh scowled at Blake defiantly and Jenny was looking pleadingly at Crystal. It was as if they expected us to change our minds or were trying to delay us.

'This is ridiculous,' said Tosh.

'Come on. On your feet and no sudden movements,' said Mary.

Eventually, they stood and approached Linda and me. We opened the doors outwards into the corridor so they pass without touching us, even though we were pretty certain the airtight suits were effective protection.

They passed through the doorway, followed closely – but not too closely – by Blake and Mary, both armed,

'Into the surgery,' said Blake. Linda and I ran across and swung the doors inwards.

'This is crazy, Blake. There's nothing wrong with me. Ask me anything,' said Tosh.

'Inside, please,' said Mary. 'Sit down over by the operating table.'

Once they were seated, Blake said, 'Right. The pallet please, Mark.'

I walked to the common room and collected a portable pallet of food and water, wheeling it into the surgery where I deposited it and withdrew the trolley.

'There are enough supplies for two weeks there, Tosh,' I said. 'We've disconnected your water supply and once we've closed these doors, we'll be sealing you in. Your air conditioning is independent of the rest of Moonbase so there's no way for any of your parasites to get out.'

'Crystal,' shouted Jenny, 'you can't let them lock me in here. Please, Crystal, *please!*'

Crystal didn't reply. We closed the door and I used a leak-patching gun to make the seal airtight.

'Computer, this is Commander Blake.'

'Yes, Blake.'

'And this is deputy Commander Mary.'

'Yes, Mary.'

'Computer, emergency override of passwords. All passwords used by John, Jenny and Roy to be deleted on our authority,' said Blake.

'Command accepted. Mary, do you concur?' asked the computer.

'I concur,' said Mary.

'Command executed, Mary and Blake.'

'Computer, lock the surgery door and unlock the doors to ward one and ward two,' said Blake.

'Surgery locked and doors to ward one and ward two unlocked, Blake,' said the computer. There was no point in locking Roy in the ward any longer.

Blake signalled for us to return to the comdome and we told Neil at NASA that the plan had been executed without incident. We all breathed a sigh of relief.

'Be sure to wear suits continually,' said Neil.

'We will,' replied Crystal.

We unsealed our facemasks and tucked our self-sealing gloves into the pockets.

Some routine could return to our lives now, but we needed to remain vigilant in case of some violent breakout, so suits were essential. It would only take a minute to reseal them. We were still isolated, a quarter of a million miles from Earth, with no idea how the situation could be resolved.

35 Imprisoned

It was not pleased. It had been outmanoeuvred by the humans. It had been forced to take an emergency decision, but it might be too early. This was not good. Two of it were extremely weak, barely alive. It didn't like trusting to luck, but it had to; it had no other alternative. If its spur of the moment decision in the Comdome had been premature, there might still be later opportunities. However, it was dealing with an intelligent species. If it gave the humans time to work the problem, the danger could only grow worse.

36 Survival Struggle

We were safer, but owing to our reduced numbers, Crystal's distress at losing her partner and our inability to return to normal duties, the atmosphere remained uncomfortable.

I couldn't continue to survey craters without a partner with geological knowledge. Crystal could step in, but that would stop her work on the internal structure of moon rocks. Any external work would leave the remaining healthy crew vulnerable. I felt redundant until the problem was resolved and a replacement team could arrive from Earth. I had no confidence we were really safe either.

I didn't think they could break down the door from inside without the correct chemical and we had checked the stock report to make certain there was no acid-gun in Tosh's stores. I wished we had another biologist among the crew. The entity in the safe could then have been examined, but Jenny was the only one with the necessary skills. Three of our colleagues were possessed by some sort of alien creature.

Of course, the larger importance of the entities was lost amid the fear they created. The fact we'd discovered an alien creature living on the surface of our own moon was phenomenal. We should be rejoicing and investigating its biological origins, discovering where it had come from, whether or not it was indigenous and, given that it was intelligent, how to communicate with it.

Instead, we'd imprisoned it and were living in fear of it finding a way out of the sealed surgery area. It was the entity's fault, of course. It had chosen to take us over instead of communicating with us. Maybe that was its only function. Should we try to reason with it?

NASA had spoken to the Chinese, so they were aware of our problem and were put on the alert in case they encounter an entity themselves. They, too, had a doctor, but their scanning equipment would be no better than ours as regarded finding a tiny creature hiding within a body. We'd found nothing during Roy's scan. Another reason for speaking to the Chinese was in case we were overwhelmed by the alien entity and it attempted to travel to the Chinese habitat in a buggy, something none of us wanted to contemplate.

The day passed. We knew from experience that the creature was now capable of dividing, which made us more conscious of the potential danger. We tried to do ordinary things, simple duties which didn't involve us being alone or giving us time to brood. Linda and I spent some time in the Garage, checking that everything was charged, the suits were in place and the tools all present, clean and correct.

While Blake, Linda and I were talking in the comdome, Crystal and Mary headed to the biodome and returned with eight eggs. Blake cooked us all his speciality spicy omelettes.

Later in the day, Blake and Crystal stayed in the comdome with Mary, who was on duty until the next morning. Linda and I returned to my cabin to lose ourselves in each other's arms. The danger which now hung over Moonbase, had rekindled our love.

- o O o -

The next morning, Linda and I suited up and were about to leave my cabin when we heard strange noises.

'What's that?' Linda whispered.

'Sounds like something being smashed.'

'Better seal our suits.'

'Yes, best be safe,' I said.

We closed our face plates and pulled on the gloves which self-sealed around our wrists.

What on Earth was happening? Surely they couldn't break through the sealed surgery door. Perhaps they'd found a sledgehammer in one of the surgery lockers.

'Okay?' she asked.

'Let's go. Keep alert.'

We stepped out into the corridor. I saw the crowbar come down on Linda's head too late to stop it and she crumpled to the floor. I grabbed the man's arm as he tried to hit me with a baseball-bat action. God, it was Roy! How the hell had he got out?

We wrestled over the crowbar until I managed to wrench it from his grasp, but then his fist slammed into the side of my head, dazing me.

I raised my arms in self-defence and he tried to grab and twist them to keep me still but, now that both of us were on the floor, I managed to roll over and kick out at him, striking him somewhere in the ribs. He cried out and I kneeled and struck him twice in the face. He groaned and attempted to rise, by which time I had found the crowbar and struck him as hard as I could sideways across the head. His head tilted sickeningly to one side and then he fell to the floor. He was probably unconscious, but after the way he'd struck Linda, I didn't much care if I'd killed him.

Linda was rising, somewhat unsteadily, to her feet.

'Your helmet okay?' I asked.

She looked at her wrist monitor. 'Says I'm still sealed.'

'Me too,' I panted, trying to regain my breath.

We stood, leaning against each other. 'How'd he get out?' she asked.

'No idea, but look, the surgery door is open. Someone's melted the seal from the outside. Blake, Mary or Crystal must have been one of them,' I said.

'But we checked them,' said Linda.

We made our way stealthily to the comdome door and peered through the oval door windows. A scene of destruction greeted us. Blake and Tosh were slamming every piece of equipment with sledge hammers.

'They're trying to cut us off,' said Linda.

'We're the only two left,' I said. 'Come on!'

I grabbed Linda's hand and we raced along the corridor to the biodome. We looked through the doors into the tunnel. No one.

We entered the corridor and ran the length of it, stopping to look through the windows into the dome itself.

'Can't see anyone,' I said.

We entered and listened. Just the isolated clucking of the chickens.

'Quick!' I said and pulled on Linda's arm as we dashed to the admin room, opened the safe and checked the entity was still in the container. I shook it.

'Is it alive?' she asked.

'Can't tell. It falls around the cylinder if you turn it, look. Might be dead.'

'Doesn't matter, bring it anyway. Let's go,' she said, and we ran back into the corridor.

At the habitat end of the central Moonbase corridor, we could see Roy, unmoving in the distance. There were still crashing noises coming from the Comdome. We had a short window of opportunity to carry out a hastily-sketched plan B. We hurried to put it into action.

'Computer,' I said quietly, 'where are Mary, Crystal and Jenny?'

'Mary and Crystal are in the common room. Jenny is in the garage, Mark.'

When we arrived at the garage, I opened the door cautiously.

'Computer, drop the garage pressure to 25 percent,' said Linda as the door closed behind us.

'Garage pressure reducing to 25 percent, Linda.'

'Why?' I asked.

'No one else will be able to open the garage door and, with any luck, Jenny will give away her location. These suits blow up a bit in low pressure but can tolerate 25 percent if you're careful.'

'Clever girl,' I said and readied the crowbar.

Buggy two's door was open. Suddenly, Jenny tumbled out, sprawling on the floor, gasping for breath.

'Computer, repressurise garage,' she called.

'Computer, ignore Jenny's command,' said Linda.

'Garage pressure continuing to reduce to 25 percent, Linda.'

I walked up to Jenny and swung the crowbar violently at her head. Now was no time for holding back. She fell over and I looked into her eyes. They were lifeless.

'She's out cold. What was she doing?' I asked.

'Look. In the doorway of the buggy. Supplies!' said Linda. 'They were planning to head to the Chinese habitat.'

'Yes. Looks like it.' I lifted Jenny's body and threw it into buggy two, closing the door behind her. At 25 percent air pressure she'd not regain consciousness, but neither would she die.

'Can you open buggy three's door, with this low pressure?'

'Think so,' I said. I turned the handle, but it stopped at the failsafe catch. I leaned against it with all my weight and took the handle past the safety point. The door swung open, almost taking me with it.

'Quick, inside and power up,' said Linda.

'Cavor, power up and prepare to depart,' I said.

'Powering up and preparing to depart,' said Cavor.

Inside the buggy, we closed the door, pressurised, climbed out of our swollen airtight suits and put on our lightweight pressure suits.

Once we were sealed in, Linda depressurised the buggy, climbed out and gave the computer the command to open the outer garage doors.

She then ran over to the door as it rose, and pulled a heavy tool chest into the doorway. It would stop the door closing and slow any pursuit.

It only took a couple of minutes. She climbed back in and I drove the buggy carefully out of the garage, taking care not to hit the tool chest.

We were soon bouncing along at 15 miles per hour. We were on our way.

37 Victory

Three versions of it waited quietly in the surgery.

Two other, extremely weak entities clung beneath the seats Tosh and Jenny had occupied in the comdome. By morning they'd be strong enough to act, but there was danger in waiting until then. They were two, but the humans were three in this room.

About five in the morning, one entity slid down the stem of the chair, across the floor and up the stem of the chair occupied by Crystal. She was wearing an airtight suit, so it couldn't act. It climbed slowly onto the underside of the arm of the chair. Crystal was entering data. Her hand was exposed.

Meantime, the other slithered slowly across the floor to where Blake was sleeping on the couch. This was much easier. It climbed the leg, made its way along the couch in the manner of a slug. The man's face was exposed. A touch was all it needed and then it was inside the cheek, following blood vessels to the spine and up into the brain. Blake didn't even have time to react.

Crystal finished the data she was inputting. She sat back. She sat back. Her hand touched something cold and wet. There was instant pain, she saw it and violently shook her arm, trying to dislodge it, but too late. It was through her skin, following the veins of her forearm, shoulder, neck and head. All over. One to go in here and then there'd need to be a recuperation. Must get to Roy and extract his divided parasite. Quiet now.

It was experienced now; controlling its subjects was not such a problem as it had been with Roy. Blake and Crystal rose, silently. Crystal went to the emergency cabinet which contained a sealant gun and complementary acid gun. She selected the acid gun and the two of them eased their way out of the Comdome, taking great care not to allow the doors to make a sound.

They crossed to the surgery and unsealed the left door. Roy emerged and they followed him back to the comdome.

Mary was stretched out on the temporary bunk which had been brought in by Mark the previous day. As Roy approached her, something must have woken her. She stared at him, gasped, pulled down her mask and leapt to her feet.

'Come on, Mary, there's nowhere to run,' the Roy entity said as she struggled to pull on the self-sealing gloves. She ran towards the toilet. It knew it mustn't allow her to get inside as she could lock it and communicate with Mark or Linda on the personal intercom.

The mad dash ended with her half in and half out of the toilet cubicle. She was trying to close the door and Roy had his arm inside the door, hanging on to the slider-lock. Mary attempted to dislodge him. In the process she reached higher up his arm. Roy tore at the self-sealing glove and exposed Mary's skin. In less than a second, one of the entities left his wrist, made contact with Mary's arm and she was possessed!

Six down, two to go.

Crystal, Mary and Blake slumped onto the couch to recover while Roy, Tosh and Jenny found tools they could use to smash the com consoles.

Once that was well underway and Moonbase was cut off from NASA, Roy headed into the corridor, picked up a crowbar from the garage and waited outside Mark's room. No one could open a personal cabin from outside, so he waited by the door.

It would be a simple matter for six of them to overpower Mark and Linda. The entity in the safe would take over Mark, and Linda would be imprisoned until one of them could divide.

It had outguessed the humans. Victory was certain.

38 On The Run

'Linda Fuller calling LOP. Over.'

'LOP receiving, Linda. What can I do for you? Over,' answered the computer on the Lunar Orbiting Platform.

'Anyone on board, LOP?'

'No. A Chinese team left for the habitat yesterday. The next flight is to bring two of the Moonbase crew up to LOP for transfer back to Earth, Linda. A crew of two is due to arrive in seven days to transfer to Moonbase.'

'Confirm there's an Orion docked, LOP.'

'There are two Orions at the station. One is docked, Linda.'

'Thank you, LOP. Please let me have telemetry for your current orbit.'

'Transferring telemetry, Linda.'

'LOP, prepare for an unscheduled arrival from Moonbase today.'

'What is the nature of the unscheduled arrival, Linda?'

'Mark Noble and Linda Fuller are returning to Earth early, LOP.'

'Understood, Linda.'

'Can you relay this conversation by secure message to Neil Weston at NASA, please, LOP.'

'Message being relayed, Linda.'

'They'll be in a flap when they get that,' I said.

'How long to the Dragonstar, Mark?'

'Fifteen minutes.'

'Right. Peace and quiet please, Mark, while I work on these telemetry figures.'

'Okay.'

The surface here was a little less flat than the region around Moonbase and I needed to concentrate to avoid small craters. They didn't appear much of a problem, but if the wheels hit them from one side or the other, they really tossed you about.

The radio came to life again. *'Mark, Linda, this is Blake. Return to Moonbase immediately.'*

'Ignore it,' said Linda.

Blake repeated his call several times, then the airwaves went quiet until the LOP computer called us. *'Linda, LOP here. Neil has received your message and will speak to you when you are aboard Dragonstar.'*

'Thank you, LOP,' said Linda.

NASA could only contact the buggies through the Moonbase comdome and, judging from what we saw, the comdome would be of no use to anyone.

'LOP, do not respond to any calls from any Moonbase personnel except me or Mark Noble,' said Linda.

'That will need NASA approval, Linda,' said LOP.

'LOP, tell Neil Weston what I have requested.'

'Contacting Neil Weston with that information, Linda.'

'Do you think NASA will realise what's happening?' Linda asked.

'They'll have tried to speak to Moonbase and have got no reply, so, yes, probably,' I said.

'Linda, Mark. Mary here. I'm okay. I'm following Blake's buggy. Don't leave without me.'

'Ha. Do they think we're stupid?' said Linda. 'They must be calling us from buggies, so they're definitely coming after us.'

'Without doubt. The tool chest blocking the door will have slowed them down. Can they stop us leaving?' I asked.

'Yes, if we're not in the last throes of the countdown.'

'What can they do?'

'A buggy could pull Dragonstar over using a tow rope,' said Linda.

'What can I do to stop that?'

'I really don't know. Keep your pedal to the metal and shut up while I work on the maths.'

I squeezed the last fraction of speed out of the buggy's motors and we tore across the surface, driving directly through all but the worst surface obstructions. Dragonstar appeared on the horizon.

'I can see her,' I said. 'Five minutes.'

'We need to decamp and get into the ship as quickly as possible. I've got checklists to run through, so you deal with everything you can,' said Linda.

'Can you take shortcuts through the checklists?'

'Only if you want us to miss LOP by a few thousand miles. You just keep everything off my back and let me get on with it.'

'Okay,' I said. I squeezed her hand and concentrated on avoiding the worst of the craters and boulders.

'Cavor, reduce air pressure to zero,' I said.

'Reducing air pressure to zero, Mark.'

When we came to a halt, there would now be no delay in opening the hatch and getting out.

A few minutes later I swung the buggy around so that the door faced the Dragonstar.

The ship stood about thirteen metres tall. The top section was shaped like an Apollo capsule. The distance from the nose to the jets was about nine metres. The whole craft sat on four legs which splayed out during landing for stability. The design of the legs allowed for the craft to land badly and still remain in a launch position.

Linda was out of the hatch almost before we'd stopped. She bunny-hopped across to the leg which had the ladder attached, and climbed rapidly to the main hatch on the Dragonstar, ten metres above the moon's surface. She unlocked the door carefully and swung it back to the holding bracket on the hull.

I grabbed the sample cylinder and our airtight suits and quickly followed her into the capsule, throwing the suits into a locker and placing the cylinder into a luggage holder made of netting. I returned to the door and looked into the distance. No sign of our pursuers yet. I could hear Linda mumbling to herself over the open suit radio channel as she went through the vital checklists.

'Dragonstar here. Do you read me, LOP?'

'I read you, Linda.'

'Transfer LOP orbit telemetry into Dragonstar computer, LOP.'

'Transferring telemetry, Linda.'

I heard her flicking switches and confirm her own responses to the checklists. I heard her say, 'Pre-launch check list complete,' which was promising – and welcome, as two buggies finally appeared over the horizon and were now speeding towards us. On the moon, the horizon is only a mile and half away. They'd be here far too soon.

'I can see them. They'll be here in six minutes. Can I help?'

'No,' Linda replied curtly.

There was nothing on the Dragonstar I could use as a weapon. I slipped down the ladder, into the buggy and grabbed the heavy adjustable wrench. I wished we'd brought a taser, but there'd been no time. I also took some sampling containers. If the worst came to the worst, I could throw them. I climbed back into the capsule and turned to see both buggies just a few hundred metres away. It's amazing how quickly objects approach on the moon.

'Link Dragonstar computer with LOP computer,' said Linda.

'Computers linked, Linda.'

'Check the Dragonstar trajectory against your telemetry, LOP.'

There was a short silence, then, *'Telemetry matches, Linda.'*

'How much time, Mark?' she called over her shoulder.

'They're here,' I said.

I watched the hatch open on buggy two, then two suited figures descended the ladder. Blake and Roy. They approached the main ladder attached to Dragonstar and began to climb. I hurled a sampling container down. It caught Blake on the shoulder and he lost his grip on the ladder. He didn't fall, but he was hanging on precariously. He soon recovered and started up again. Taking careful aim, I threw a second sampler and caught him fair and square on the faceplate.

He looked up at me and shouted something, but his suit radio must have been off. A third container hit his arm and a fourth his helmet again. He was still climbing.

'How long, Linda?'

'One minute and you can shut up,' she said.

Blake was now on the vertical section of the ladder to the hatch. I waited until his head appeared above the opening and swung the wrench with all my might.

The visor split and a plume of air shot out of it. He lost his grip and fell, hitting Roy on the way down. Both men crumpled under the craft.

'Right. Shut hatch and take a seat, quick,' shouted Linda.

I closed the door and used a piece of cable to tie the handle to the nearest bracket, making it, I hoped, impossible to open from outside.

'Computer, pressurise,' shouted Linda.

'Pressurising, Linda,' said the ship's computer.

'How're you doing, Mark? Ten seconds to blast off.'

'Okay. I'm just belting up.'

'Five, four, three, two, one, ignition,' she said.

I felt the vessel shake as the main motor fired.

'Lift-off,' Linda said.

The vessel climbed rapidly, far more rapidly than a lift-off on Earth. We'd made it. We'd survived the assault. If Blake and Roy had still been beneath the jet they'd likely have been fried. I guessed I'd killed Blake when I punctured his visor, anyway, but the entity would probably have climbed out of his body and survived on the moon's surface.

'LOP. We've lifted off,' said Linda.

'Copy you, Linda.'

The ride was extremely smooth. There was no air pressure to battle through, so very little sense of the power which was carrying us up into lunar orbit. It felt strange experiencing stronger gravity again. We suddenly weighed half of what we did on Earth, but three times what we did on the moon.

'Well done. You were brilliant, Linda,' I said as the engine cut. In free fall once again, we coasted towards the rendezvous orbit.

'Phew. Exhausting. Just hope I didn't make any mistakes.'

'How long to LOP?'

'Unfortunately, the optimum blast-off should've been twenty minutes later. We'll be in orbit in three minutes, but it'll take a couple of hours for the platform to catch up with us.'

'We can relax, then,' I said, taking my helmet off.

'A little. Soon we'll have docking to worry about, but for now we need to call Neil. Heaven knows what he'll say about us abandoning Moonbase.'

'We had no choice.'

'No. Can't believe the entity got the other six of us,' Linda said.

'I suppose Mary was infected.'

'No doubt about it. It was just another ploy to stop us. We were lucky,' I said.

'I can't believe how intelligent they are. Frightening.'

We squeezed each other's hands.

39 Failure

It needed to isolate Moonbase in order to strengthen all of its components and learn more about the humans and their technology.

It began dismantling and smashing the communication equipment. The last thing it wanted was for the remaining two humans to be able to tell NASA that they were the only two left.

It discovered from Blake's mind that the humans' long conversation with NASA the previous evening had advised them how to isolate the infected people in the surgery. Only its quick thinking allowed it to leave the two very weak entities on the Comdome chairs, otherwise it really would have been imprisoned.

Leaving only Roy to stand guard over the other two humans was a mistake. Roy's entity had quickly re-established Roy's consciousness, but it had lost many minutes.

It soon became clear that Mark and Linda were trying to escape. Blake, Tosh, Crystal and Mary dashed to the garage and found that there was reduced pressure inside, making it impossible to open the door. Then the pressure dropped to zero, meaning that the humans must be leaving in a buggy. When the garage pressure didn't return to normal, it realised the humans must have blocked the outer door to stop it closing.

Tosh and Blake dashed to the EVA dome, quickly put on pressure suits and bunny-hopped around the outside of Moonbase. It was all taking time.

When they arrived at the garage, they found the door had been propped open. The tool box was quickly moved, pressure returned, and Roy, Crystal and Mary entered from the corridor. Jenny had been hurt, but her parasite was carrying out repairs to her skull from the inside, synthesising calcium from the blood stream and rebuilding the damaged synapses.

It took a while to sort out their situation. Then Blake and Roy took one buggy, Tosh and Mary the other, and they set off in pursuit.

How much of a start had the humans got? It examined the wheel tracks. The freshest set didn't head towards the Chinese habitat, so they must be heading for the Dragonstar.

The chase began. It must stop them leaving.

- o O o -

The humans' buggy was already at the Dragonstar and the hatch stood open. One person was visible in the doorway – probably Mark, as Linda was the designated pilot.

Blake climbed the ladder towards the hatch, but when he reached it, Mark smashed his faceplate. Air rushed out and Blake fell to the ground, taking Roy with him.

Roy saw the hatch shut and knew lift-off would be imminent. He pulled Blake clear of the jet and slapped an emergency patch over the visor. The patch quickly bulged outwards as suit pressure recovered. Would Blake's entity be able to repair any damage to the body? If they'd realised time was so short, one of them could have left its host, attached itself to the Dragonstar and travelled into orbit with the humans, but it all happened too quickly.

The Dragonstar took off. Although the two hosts and buggy three were blown over, they survived. The second buggy, with Tosh and Mary on board, arrived and they helped Blake back into buggy one. The Dragonstar was disappearing from view. They had failed.

The humans on Earth would now be plotting their downfall.

Its original plan to travel to the Chinese habitat would have to be a priority.

The two buggies returned towards Moonbase, leaving buggy three abandoned on its side on the lunar surface.

40 Rendezvous

'What happened? What went wrong?' asked Neil from NASA.

'We think they must've left a parasite in the comdome when we locked them up in the surgery. Once they'd taken over Crystal, Blake or Mary, it would've been easy to open the surgery from outside and take over the remaining two,' I said.

'Computer, LOP, I've activated automatic approach,' said Linda, touching a few symbols on the control board to start the autonomous docking with the Lunar Orbiting Platform.

'Automatic approach in progress, Linda,' said the computer, echoed by the LOP computer a few seconds later.

The Dragonstar would now line itself up with one of the LOP docking ports.

'We've warned the Chinese and advised them to use lethal force to stop any of our people entering their habitat,' said Neil.

'We reckon that the entities can get out of them, so even a dead human doesn't mean there isn't a parasite hiding somewhere. That's how we got caught out,' I said.

'Yes. We'll let them know.'

'Mary said she hadn't been infected and asked us to wait to take her with us. We assumed it was a ruse and she didn't call us again,' I said.

'Okay. I think you made the correct decision.'

'That one we encountered at Timocharis Delta must've been there for centuries, in a vacuum and buried in dust. I'm beginning to think they're indestructible. We might have to abandon the moon to them if they're common.'

'I hope it doesn't come to that. There must be a way to destroy them. The mine at Copernicus is planned for early next year. We wouldn't want to cancel that project.'

'No, we've been watching inbound unmanned spacecraft flying overhead during the last few weeks.'

'And they'll be almost continuous until January,' said Neil.

'I have one of the entities in the airtight sample container. We could eject it on a sun-bound trajectory, or we could bring it with us.'

'Didn't realise you'd brought it with you. The container's secure?' asked Neil.

'Blake said it was airtight. Its lid is securely fastened.'

'Okay. I need to take advice. I'll get back to you about it.'

'One metre,' said LOP.

'Copy that,' said Linda.

'We're just about to dock, Neil. I'll get back to you when we've checked out the Orion,' I said.

'Roger that, Mark. Out.'

The Dragonstar shuddered as the docking probe entered its receptacle on the Lunar Orbiting Platform. Automatic clasps would now seal the ship to the station.

'Well done, Linda.'

'I'm shattered!' she said, puffing out her cheeks and stretching. 'Could do with a rest after that. You handle the docking checks.'

Thirty minutes later, the docking was confirmed "hard". I opened the hatch at the front of Dragonstar, allowing us into the space platform.

It was cold. 'LOP, raise temperature to 23 degrees,' I said.

'Temperature rising, Mark.'

We floated in through the docking node and into the main communal area where we could get out of our suits and make ourselves a coffee and a bite to eat. Linda wrapped a net and blanket around herself and curled up to rest. I heated two coffee pouches and rifled through the meal supplies.

'What do you fancy to eat, Linda?'

'Something calorific. Chilli con carne?'

I checked, 'Yep. I'll join you with that.'

I tossed an energy bar in her direction as I heated coffee packs which we sucked upon eagerly as we floated side by side and waited for the microwave to ping.

'You were magnificent, Linda.'

'Thank you, kind sir, but I think NASA will frown at the shortcuts I took before lift-off, when they check the recording.'

'It got us here.'

'I don't think you realise the sort of mess we could have been in if I'd got any of those telemetry readings wrong and I didn't double check any of them!' she said, anxiously.

'Never doubted you.'

'I can't ever remember being so frightened as when I saw you clobber Blake. I had visions of hordes of blue blobs climbing in through the hatch,' she said.

'I feel dreadful that I might have killed him.'

'You had to stop him, Mark.'

'I know, but the real Blake was inside that body somewhere and he knocked Roy off when he fell. Might have killed them both when the jet fired.'

'Probably not,' said Linda. 'It isn't hugely powerful. Getting off the moon is nothing like the take-off from Earth. They'll be okay if they weren't directly under us. It's not a whole lot more powerful than a hovercraft jet.'

'Don't know why I care, really. It wasn't them anymore,' I said as the microwave pinged and I took out our meals.

'No, but they were our friends. Now they're as good as dead. Could have been us, too,' Linda said.

We sat in silence for a moment. Roy had been a special friend, but so was Tosh. They were all gone now. 'Maybe NASA will find a way to extract the entities from them,' I said.

'We can hope,' Linda said as we peeled back the tops of our containers and sampled the contents.

'Really good,' I said. 'Hadn't realised how hungry I was.'

'We missed breakfast and it's two in the afternoon now,' she said.

After our lunch, we let NASA know our status and tried to get a couple of hours rest now that the LOP was up to temperature. I pulled the net around us and exhaustion soon caused the inevitable result.

- o O o -

The terror we'd experienced during the fight, the escape and being pursued had its effect on me. Linda, too, had been totally exhausted. We slept for six hours. When we awoke, we were warm and loosely entangled. Relief took over and we freed ourselves from the net, hugging, kissing and consoling each other. It's very rare to be alone with one other person in orbit; even rarer, probably unique, for it to be a couple in love. It was a privilege which should, most certainly, not be wasted! Almost imperceptibly, but inevitably, consoling morphed into desiring. We were soon naked and discovering that there was no better way than freefall lovemaking to vanquish all the fear, tension, stresses and strains we'd encountered. It allowed us to shut out the trauma and worry, at least for an hour or so.

At eleven in the evening we needed to get serious. We dressed in our Orion flight suits to begin prepping the spacecraft for the return to Earth. There'd been no more news from the moon, via NASA or the Chinese.

Our flight would take around three days, leaving lunar orbit at a relatively slow speed and falling towards Earth, allowing gravity to accelerate us to 25,000 miles per hour for re-entry, always the scariest part of any mission.

Orion was built for up to six astronauts. It is quite spacious and less claustrophobic than the Apollos from the early days of moon exploration. Normally there'd be two qualified Orion pilots, but we didn't have that luxury. I was familiar with the systems and had done some simulation training, but Linda would be pretty much on her own in making sure everything went smoothly.

I contacted NASA.

'Our friend is still lifeless,' I said as I examined the strange piece of jelly inside the cylinder. 'Do we bring it or dump it?'

'Double check the screw top is firmly closed,' said Ken White, our Orion mission controller.

'Sealed tight,' I said.

'When you splash down. Do not open the hatch. We'll fly the whole thing to the nearest base. We can then decontaminate as you emerge,' said Ken.

'It will be in the storage net behind the commander's seat,' I said.

'Sounds fine.'

'Permission to separate, NASA?' asked Linda.

'You've a go for separation,' said Ken White.

'Separating, LOP,' said Linda.

'Disconnected, Linda,' said LOP.

The Orion was now drifting slowly away from LOP. We were both strapped into our seats. I had a view of the moon from my window. I wondered if we would ever return. My mission on the surface still had eight weeks to run. It was different for Linda, as she was a designated Dragonstar pilot, so filled in on general duties at Moonbase or on board the LOP Gateway between ferrying people and supplies to and from the surface.

I felt the spacecraft turn and weightlessness vanished as Linda made some orbital adjustments.

We waited patiently for the next thirty minutes until we were in the right part of LOP's orbit to fire our motor to put us into the Earth injection orbit.

The rocket fired for several minutes, then cut out. Linda checked with NASA; our trajectory was perfect. In a little under three days we'd be home.

41 Effort

It sensed that something had changed. There had been an acceleration, presumably into orbit. That was followed by a period of weightlessness. It only sensed two humans nearby. Where were its other components? Although it had been captured, it still possessed a large amount of the knowledge from its original host, the Roy thing. It sensed what was happening around it.

For it to be in the possession of these two humans, something must have gone wrong on the moon. The objective to reach the Earth, must have been passed to it.

It was in a spacecraft in microgravity. There had been a firing of a motor and now they were in freefall again. It had to assume they were heading to the Earth. How long would it take? Could it escape?

The cylinder had a glass side, but it was almost as strong as the steel. It braced itself against the metal and pushed the lid. No movement. Perhaps it unscrewed. Bracing again it tried to turn the top of the device one way – nothing – then the other. There was a very slight movement, but it wouldn't turn enough.

It examined the lid. This wasn't a lid, this was a plate which slid in and out of a slot in the cylinder. No wonder it couldn't be moved, the top of the cylinder must have screwed down upon it. So why did the plate move at all?

If it braced itself and pushed upwards, it moved about half a millimetre. It pushed a tendril into the space. It went along the width of the cylinder's wall and encountered the actual lid. The lid had a screw thread.

Push and squeeze! Compress and lubricate. Try again. The tendril got into the mesh of the thread. With a tremendous effort, it followed its feeler, slithering through the tiny gap which was even smaller than the space between the tyre and wheel of the buggy in which it had first concealed itself.

Advance, squash, shorten, shrink, stretch, constrict, shrivel, slide, slip and wriggle. Around and around the thread, occupying the tiniest space as it followed the steel ridge and groove.

Two hours later, the tendril sensed air. Resembling a gelatinous glob of transparent oil, it pulled itself around the grooves until it was outside the cylinder. It was free.

Two beings were loosely restrained in harnesses. It was too weak to possess both of them. It would have to take one of them now and then the second. Which one first?

What were their functions in this craft? The male was sleeping. The female was interacting with the control panel. Was she the pilot? It reached back into its knowledge of Roy. Who were the females? One was already occupied, that was Jenny, so forget her. Crystal was a scientist, Mary a geologist and Linda a pilot. Was this Linda?

It remembered Mark visiting Roy. This was Mark. The female who came with him was Linda. So, the female must be Linda. It didn't want to distract the ship's pilot, so Mark ought to be the first victim.

It eased itself across some webbing on the wall, making its way to the back of Mark's seat.

It wished it knew the timing of the flight. Would it have time to take them both over? If it had five or six days, it would be more sensible to possess the female. If it were short of time, then the male.

Why didn't they speak? It needed clues as to the duration of the flight. It decided to conceal itself at the back of Mark's couch and await developments. Why didn't they speak?

42 Almost Home

'Was that another course correction?' I asked, emerging from my catnap.

'Yes, should be the last. We're accelerating rapidly now, somewhere in the region of 17,000 miles per hour. Re-entry in about an hour,' Linda replied.

'Hello, Orion 32c, come in, over,' said Mission Control.

'Orion 32c here. Course correction complete,' said Linda.

'We've just been checking trajectories and you should come down about fifty miles north of Bermuda. The Donald J. Trump is steaming towards the splashdown area. We've decided to leave you in the capsule during recovery. Sorry, but we want to move you to a quarantine location before opening the hatch in case it broke free somehow.'

'Guessed as much,' said Linda. 'How long from recovery to destination? I'm not a good sailor.'

'Ha ha. You fly to and from the moon for a living, but you're worried about a bit of sea-sickness?'

'I know it's strange, but there you go. How long?'

'We should have you into the facility in Wilmington within a few hours.'

'Roger that.'

'Didn't know you got ill at sea,' I said.

'Don't you remember those splashdown exercises we did in training?'

'Oh, yes, but you weren't actually sick.'

'I suppose not, but I felt awful,' she said.

'What's next?'

'We separate from the service module at about three hundred miles. The final trajectory will be locked in and we'll hit the atmosphere with the heatshield protecting us. We should try to get some more rest.'

'Yes,' I said and closed my eyes again.

43 Now or Never

So, she is Linda and she is the pilot. Better not mess with her. Mark will be the victim.

Interesting that they might think it could not get out of this craft. It was sure it could find a way, but for now it must get into Mark, stealthily, and hope that Linda didn't notice any change. They were both sleeping lightly.

It made its way over the top of the seat, then down onto the rim where Mark's helmet would fit. Inside, it crossed to the garment around his neck and there was his bare skin.

It knew it had to silence him so prepared its attack. A tendril touched the neck and it was instantly inside him. In less than half a second, it had the speech centres within its control and then the motor systems.

All the time it was taking sustenance and energy from the human, strengthening itself ready for the next division. It could, of course, leave Mark and hide in the ship, but losing the source of energy would set it back. Better to stay within this human and look for opportunities later. No quarantine they could devise would be able to stop it escaping into the environment when it was ready.

44 Paralysed

I felt a pain in my neck, like an electric shock. I tried to cry out and failed, wanted to reach out to Linda, but couldn't. Whatever it was, it had me totally immobilised by its induced paralysis. I felt as if I was being squeezed and herded into a tiny space somewhere within my head.

I sensed what it was doing. It was learning how to move me. I felt my fingers, toes, knees, arms, elbows, wrist and eyelids being moved in tiny increments. It was learning how to do it without actually making noticeable movements. I wanted to look towards Linda but couldn't move my head or neck or even swivel my eyes in her direction.

I made a great effort to speak and emitted a tiny sound. The attempt was rewarded with a pain, like a red-hot needle poked into me. I didn't even know where the needle was, it was just a hot needle sticking into me somewhere. I tried again, and the pain was multiplied. Being unable to cry out meant that the scream I had wanted to utter was trapped within me. There could be no release. Is this what the others had experienced? Were they similarly imprisoned within their bodies? If so, then Blake might have welcomed death when I smashed his faceplate.

Is that where the entity came from? Had it been somewhere on the outside of the Dragonstar and found its way in?

My God! It answered my thoughts! It was the entity which was in the sample cylinder. But that was airtight. How did it get out? Did it smash the glass section? No. It crawled around the thread of the lid. How? How could something find its way along a groove which didn't even allow air to pass? It could squeeze itself to the height and width smaller than a molecule of air.

The capsule wouldn't hold it. It could find its way out of here and into the environment. The Earth was in trouble. This was an existential threat. The entity was unstoppable. I needed to tell Earth to destroy us or to tell Linda to put us into a steeper descent, so we'd burn up on re-entry. Red-hot needles, hundreds of them, told me what the entity thought of that idea.

   I could do nothing. I could tell no one. Linda needed to see my eyes. Only then would she know what had to be done.

45 Journey's End

'Wake up, Mark. Time's getting short. We're through the outer Van Allen belts.'

'Right, what is our status?' the entity asked on my behalf.

'Twenty minutes to re-entry. Velocity 25,000 miles per hour. Approaching the inner Van Allen belts. The radiation will peak a few minutes before we hit the atmosphere. Helmets on,' said Linda.

I had no control at all, yet my hand lifted the helmet and slotted it onto the neck ring. It wasn't an easy task, which told me how effectively it was in control. Linda could no longer see my eyes even if she did look at me. I tried to speak again. I managed a grunt, which resulted in a shower of red-hot needles.

'Mission Control, we're in the inner Van Allen belts now. Radio blackout shortly. See you in the Bermuda Triangle,' said Linda.

'Ha ha, copy that, don't get lost. See you guys soon,' replied Mission Control.

I was fighting to make a sound. The entity was doing everything in its power to stop me, but I was managing the odd grunt. Not loud enough for Linda to notice.

Then breakthrough. 'Linda,' I managed to say. Pain hit me, but it wasn't as targeted. I tried again. 'Infected.'

It hadn't been able to stop me speaking when I used all of my will power and concentration.

'Sorry, Mark. What was that?'

'Infected. Am infected,' it couldn't stop me, but I felt it trying to shut down my speech centres. It was as if there was a miniscule tunnel between my mind and my voice and I was able to speak through it. Why couldn't it? What was happening? My entire body was bathed in pain.

'You're not infected,' she said.

'Yes. Got me. Got out of sampler!'

'No, no, nooo! It can't have!'

It was getting a grip of me again. I struggled to get the words out. 'Destroy us, Linda. Burn us up. Only hope!' It was furious and enveloped me with the experience of an acid bath. I cried out in pain.

'Can't, Mark. Too late. I can no longer control orientation. It's all automatic now until splash down. You're dreaming. You can't be infected.'

I could no longer speak. I could move my arms. Its control was definitely fading, but it was concentrating on stopping me speaking. It was angry. Pain rattled around my body, as if my arms and legs were being crushed or torn off. Too much pain, too much! I lost consciousness.

I awoke in time to hear Linda shout, 'Hold tight,' then felt the impact with the atmosphere. Now the Orion capsule was being buffeted and bumped as it was tossed around by the huge external forces of re-entry.

The entity was hurting me. Hurting me everywhere, random pain inflicted upon my body and mind. I couldn't stop it and couldn't scream. Then my voice returned, momentarily, and I released an agonising guttural howl.

'Mark! *Mark!*' shouted Linda as the pain overwhelmed me and I lost consciousness again.

46 Splashdown

The Orion capsule was now on a pre-programmed path. The small adjustments to keep the heat shield facing the correct way were far too numerous and rapid to be entrusted to a human being.

Linda looked at Mark and shook him. He was out cold. She was in anguish over Mark's admission that he was infected. She could do nothing. She tried to think of something, anything she could do to destroy the capsule, but there was nothing. The euthanasia valve would do no more than kill the two of them. The thing wouldn't be affected. It seemed impervious to the lack of an atmosphere. The thrusters were no longer under her control at this point in re-entry. She tried firing one which might tip the capsule over, but it didn't fire. She knew it wouldn't but had to try.

Eventually, the Orion was through the upper atmosphere and the Orion jerked and swung violently as first the drogue chute and then the main chutes were deployed.

She heard the radio crackle. 'NASA, do you copy me?' she asked.

'Copy you, Linda. Welcome home.'

'We've a problem. The entity escaped the cylinder and has infected Mark. Please advise.'

'How sure are you?'

'Mark managed to tell me. As soon as we're in the water I'll check the cylinder.'

'But the cylinder was airtight.'

'I know, but Mark was sure. He asked me to destroy the capsule, but it was too late, we were already on automatic and in radio blackout,' she said, tearfully, her self-control breaking down with the realisation they'd seriously endangered the Earth.

'What's his status now?'

'Unconscious. He let out a scream and passed out. I think it's torturing him.'

'Okay. When you're down, check the cylinder and report back to us.'

'Are we near the correct location?'

'I'll check.'

The radio went silent. Linda looked at Mark. She didn't want to remove his helmet as, for the moment, the entity was trapped inside the suit, although if it got out of the cylinder then the suit would be no real barrier.

'Hello, Linda. You are going to splashdown within half a mile of the navy vessels. They'll lift the sealed capsule by heavy-duty Chinook. You won't be taken to the battleship, but to a light cruiser which can make thirty knots.'

'Thanks, NASA. What's the shipboard time? This entity could probably divide in twenty-four hours.'

'You'll be picked up a hundred miles off Wilmington and taken to the military base where we're preparing a quarantined warehouse for your reception. You should be there in less than ten hours after we pluck you from the Atlantic.'

'Sounds good.'

'Twenty seconds to splashdown, Linda.'

The capsule hit the water, almost turned over, then righted itself. The parachute lines were cut and floatation bags inflated.

Linda quickly recovered from the rollercoaster ride. She unstrapped herself and made her way back to the storage net which held the sampler. She picked it up, peered through the glass, shook it, examined it again and put it back into storage. She made her way, unsteadily, as the capsule was rolling in the ocean swell, back to her seat, looking at Mark on the way, and strapped herself in, battling nausea.

'Hello, NASA. Cylinder definitely empty, yet still sealed.'

'So how did it get out?'

'I know it sounds crazy, but I think it must have squeezed its way around the grooves of the screw-on lid.'

'Yes. Frighteningly crazy! You didn't see any holes or cracks in the glass?'

'No, nothing like that at all. It looks perfect. It's just empty!'

'Chinook is with you. Be prepared to be hoisted.'

'Copy that. If it got out of the airtight cylinder, the capsule might not hold it either.'

'Copy that, Linda. We're already on it.'

- o O o -

A dozen hours later, the capsule was finally stationary in the quarantine facility at Wilmington.

'Opening the hatch, Linda. Stay clear,' said Michael Dredge, head of the quarantine team.

'Copy that.'

'Keep your helmet on and shut your suit inlet valves. We've doused the capsule with poison.'

'Copy that. Haven't taken it off since splashdown.' She checked the seal, closed the valves and did the same to Mark's. He was still unconscious.

The door seals clicked open, there was a slight equalisation of pressure and daylight flooded the capsule.

'Now, please step out and make your way into the cylinder to your right as you emerge.'

'Check the outside of my suit,' she said as she exited.

Three people in contamination suits examined her. They checked suit joints, under and around valves and suit plumbing, and finally behind the sun visor.

'Nothing,' said one of the men.

'It could be almost transparent and only the length of a finger,' Linda warned. 'Presumably it could stretch itself as thin as a hair.'

They checked her again and used an infrared camera to look for heat spots.

'All clear,' one said.

Linda climbed down from the platform which they'd erected outside the capsule and saw what looked like a decompression chamber standing to one side. There was a second one standing just beside it.

The inside of the chamber was very basic. A cylinder about three metres in diameter with a chair, table, bunk and chemical toilet. Michael shut her in and told her she could strip out of her flight suit.

She couldn't help but examine every bit of her suit for jelly as she shed it. Once she'd changed, she felt much safer. There was a long oval window beside the door and she watched the action outside.

Three men carried Mark out of the hatch and took him to the second chamber. Two medics, a man and a woman, wearing full quarantine gear, entered the chamber with him and the door was closed.

Linda was surprised to see what happened next. The capsule was resealed and a brown cylinder, clearly labelled with "Cyanide" plus the skull and crossbones logo, was wheeled in and connected to the atmosphere inlet valves. They were flooding the interior of the Orion with one of the most poisonous gases known to mankind.

- o O o -

Linda lived in the chamber for two days, before she was finally released and given the all clear.

'What's happening with Mark?' she asked.

'He's still being questioned,' said Michael, 'but you can move into more comfortable accommodation over in the corner of the quarantine area.' He indicated some prefabricated buildings.

- o O o -

I saw lights. I tried to open my eyes, but they were stuck closed.

'He's awake!' someone said, opening my eyes and shining a bright light into them. I squinted.

My eyes were wiped, and I opened them properly. I was in some sort of cylindrical room, with two doctors monitoring me intently. They were in full quarantine gear. My head hurt. I reached up and pressed my hand against my right temple. 'Where am I?'

'Wilmington military hospital,' said one.

'Who are you?' I asked.

'I'm Dr. Charles List and this is Dr. Rose Welch.'

'Infected by the entity. Infected,' I said.

'Is this you or it talking?' asked Dr. Welch.

I scoured my thoughts. I couldn't sense it at all. It seemed to have released me. 'Strange. I think it might have gone,' I said.

'If you were it, that's exactly what you might say,' said Dr. Welch.

'My head hurts. Can I get a couple of paracetamols?' I asked.

'You really think it's left you?' asked Dr. List.

'Can't sense it.'

'Okay. Describe what happened when it took you over,' said Dr Welch.

'I remember a sharp pain in the side of my neck. I went to shout out but couldn't. I realised it had my speech centre in its control. I tried to wave my arm at Linda and couldn't move it. God! Is Linda okay? It hasn't transferred to her, has it?'

'She's fine. She's still in quarantine, but every test shows her to be perfectly normal so far,' said Dr. List.

'What happened next? Linda said you tried to speak,' said Dr. Welch.

'I couldn't get any words out and I could feel it moving parts of my body. It moved each toe individually. I remember that in particular, because normally I can't move my smaller toes individually. Then my fingers, my joints – knee, elbow, shoulder and even my eyelids and eyes.

'Linda told me to put my helmet on and it did it for me. I was surprised at how accurate its control was. Threading a helmet onto its rim is not easy.

'I tried to shout and managed a couple of words. Linda heard them, but didn't register what I'd said. Then it hit me with a massive amount of pain.'

'Where?' asked Dr. List.

'I don't know. It seemed to be all over. Nowhere I could actually pinpoint. It was like red-hot needles. Then I told Linda I was infected. I couldn't believe it had let me get the words out. It was annoyed with me – I sensed that, but its ability to control me was fading.

'I shouted something about it having got out of the cylinder and then for Linda to try to kill us. To burn us up in the atmosphere. I realised we mustn't be allowed back to Earth with the entity on board.'

'So, why did it let you speak if it had such control?' asked Dr. List.

'I don't know. It wasn't behaving the way it had earlier. Now it was just moving around within me, making random movements of my body and showering me with pain – again, in no specific place. I think it must've been using my central nervous system.'

'Linda said you screamed and passed out,' said Dr. List.

'Yes, the pain was mounting. Hundreds of small pains, like being pricked with needles followed by burns, as if I was being showered with acid. Then it changed to really violent pain as if it was tearing off my limbs. I got the distinct impression it had lost control. All of a sudden, there was a pain as if my eyes and tongue were being ripped from my face and I let out that final scream. Next thing I knew, I woke up here. Please, can I get something for this headache?'

'Sorry, Mark, not yet,' replied Dr. List.

'Do you have any metal implants in your body?' asked Dr. Welch.

'No. Why? An MRI scan?'

'Yes. A scanner has just been delivered. We're going to move you into it,' said Dr. Welch.

They helped me out of the bed and through the door of the metal chamber. Outside was a large white truck with *Wilmington Military Hospital* on the side. The doctors supported me up the steps and through the door. My head was killing me. The MRI operator was also in full quarantine gear.

They had me lay on the MRI scanner platform and I watched the machine warming up. Soon it was revolving, ready for me to be passed through it.

- o O o -

My headache was getting worse. I could hear the doctors and operator talking as I was passed into the whirring machine.

'What's that?' asked the operator.

'Gotcha! There it is!' shouted Dr. Welch.

'Where?' asked her colleague.

'There, just inside the skull above the right temple.'

'Oh, yes. We'd better scan the rest of him just in case it's a ruse.'

The scan continued, then returned to my head.

'Hasn't moved,' said Dr. List.

'No. Wonder if it's dead. He's been complaining of a headache exactly where it is. Do you see what it looks like?' asked Dr. Welch.

'Yes. Identical, but the human two are still in the usual place and look perfectly normal,' said Dr. List.

'I'm not deaf!' I shouted. 'What the devil are you talking about?'

'All in good time, Mark,' said Dr. Welch.

Their voices dropped a level, but I could still hear them.

'What killed it, do you think?' asked Dr. List.

'It happened just after they passed through the Van Allen belts,' said Dr. Welch. 'That might have been the cause.'

'But why was this one killed and not the human pair?'

'We need to know why, that's for sure. Could be the key to how to destroy them,' said Dr. Welch.

'Need to get it out of him. I want a better look at it,' said Dr. List.

'Don't want to cut into his skull here,' said Dr. Welch. 'We're going to have to move him to the main facility. Get everyone else cleared out. We'll need three theatre nurses, but quarantine the entire hospital.'

'Are you going to tell me what's happening?' I asked loudly.

Dr. List poked his head into the tunnel and said, 'We think we know what's causing your headache. You need to be patient.'

47 The Second Hitch-Hiker

I came to. I was the only patient in a ward of twenty or more beds.

'Nurse, he's awake!' said Linda, squeezing my hand.

My head hurt. I reached up. It was bandaged.

I smiled at Linda as she came into focus, and it was returned with interest. 'Did they get it?'

'It's okay, Mark. You're okay. Here comes the surgeon, darling. I'll let him explain.'

I looked across the ward and saw the two doctors approaching.

'Mark. Nice to see you conscious. You'll feel a lot better over the next few hours,' said Dr. List.

'What did you do?' I asked.

'It was dead inside your skull. We had to cut out a section to remove it.'

'You're sure it's dead? Seriously, are you *positive*?'

'I promise you, it's dead.'

'What happened?'

'Well, that's a bit of a mystery,' replied Dr. List. 'We know the entity could cope with hard radiation from having survived, exposed on the moon's surface without protection. That would kill a normal human if we didn't have the radiation shielding in space suits and habitats.'

'Not on the surface. Under the surface, perhaps by as much as a metre or two,' I said.

'Well, still a harsh environment,' said Dr. List.

Dr. Welch took up the explanation. 'However, the radiation is rather different in nature in the Van Allen belts. They concentrate cosmic rays and energetic particles into bands formed by our electromagnetic core. The decay of neutrons caused by the cosmic ray interactions in the belts showered the entity with energetic protons. That appears to have killed it. While we can pass through them if the journey is short, it seems the entity couldn't. The outer belts weakened it, and the inner belts killed it.'

'Amazing,' I said.

'The MRI scan showed it up very clearly inside your skull. We assume that when Roy was CT scanned by Dr. MacIntosh in Moonbase, the entity used its ability to change shape to hide itself. Once dead, it was unable to hide,' said Dr. List.

'The Earth's had a near miss. These entities are lethal,' said Linda.

'Yes, we understand that. We dare not allow any more to arrive. If they knew about the Van Allen belts, they could easily take a polar re-entry approach and we'd now be fighting it in the population,' said Dr. List.

'So, what's the plan to rid the moon of them?'

'Neil Weston will be here to brief you later today,' said Dr. Welch.

'What have you done to my head?' I asked, feeling the bandages.

'You've got a one-inch-diameter hole in your skull which we've filled with a titanium plate,' replied Dr. Welch. 'The bandages can come off tomorrow. For now, we'll leave you to recover.'

'I've got a picture of the little fellow. I'll be back with it later when Mr. Weston arrives,' said Dr. List, and then the two doctors left my bedside.

Linda said, 'Just get well again, Mark. I thought I'd lost you and caused the end of the world because I couldn't crash us. If I'd known you were infected ten minutes earlier, I'd have rotated the capsule and we'd have burned up. We wouldn't be having this conversation.'

'It was only as we entered the belts that its grip upon me began to slip.'

'We're lucky to be alive,' she said.

'You'd really have done it?' I asked.

'Once I knew you were infected. Immediately. You've no idea what I've been going through, thinking it was inside you. I checked the cylinder when we'd splashed down, and it was no longer there. I expected it to infect me as soon as it had the strength. It was half a day before they got us out of the capsule.'

'Sorry, Linda.'

'All's well that ends well,' she said and squeezed my hand again.

Later, Dr. List returned, accompanied by Neil Weston. The doctor handed me a colour printout. 'Here's a picture of it,' he said.

The entity lay in a kidney dish, about seven centimetres long. It was a dull greyish-brown colour.

'Recognise it?' asked Dr. List, casually.

'Well, we only saw it in the container, where it was almost transparent,' Linda said.

'*No.* I'm not asking if you remember this particular individual, but if you recognise the object's general appearance.'

'No,' I said.

'Looks a bit like a seahorse,' said Linda.

'And what's the scientific name of a seahorse?' asked the surgeon.

'Hippo-something,' Linda said.

'Hippocampus,' I said.

'Oh, yes,' Linda said, 'the same name as the things on the top of the spine in our brains.'

'Yes,' said Dr. List. 'We've two of them and they got their name because they looked like seahorses.'

'So, is this related to our hippocampus?' I asked.

'As far as we can tell, so far, this *is* a hippocampus,' said Dr. List.

'What are you saying?' asked Linda.

'That we have two relations of this entity in our bodies. All of us, and most mammals,' the doctor replied.

'You're saying we might be related?' I exclaimed.

He continued, 'We're speculating that, at some time in the distant past these little blighters arrived on Earth and entered the brains of some mammals. We have two of them under the cerebral cortex and we think they're a vital part of memory. Without memory, intelligence is less likely. Dementia's a disease which most seriously affects the hippocampus, which gives you an idea how important it is.

There's speculation that the hippocampus gave us our intelligence, and we're now wondering if it was an ancient space traveller.'

'Why did it attack us on the moon?' I asked.

Neil took over the explanation. 'It was probably evolved to take over any animal it encountered, become part of it and help it evolve and improve. It was probably surprised to discover that Roy already had two of its relations embedded in his own brain.'

'So why do our hippocampi survive trips through the Van Allen belts?' I asked.

'Simply that it's a different type of radiation from what this entity was used to on the moon,' said Neil. 'The concentration of high-energy protons were the killers. The Van Allen belts herd them into dangerous clumps. It's why we avoid lingering within them during missions.'

'So, the humans did try to resist it on the moon, then?' asked Linda.

'Yes, but if you think about it, there could be no resistance,' said Neil. 'The scientists at NASA want to interview Mark to find out how much he was able to resist.'

'Hardly at all. It had total control, but then seemed to slip and let me speak a little,' I said.

'Yes. It was dying. If it hadn't died, the whole world would have become infected on the basis that two times two recurring becomes an enormous number within very few divisions. You can't resist, because the hippocampus becomes the new "you", just as was the case with your colleagues at Moonbase.'

'But I'd *never* have given up fighting,' I protested.

'Never's a long time, Mark,' said Dr. List. 'I think the old Vogon saying, "Resistance is useless!" would certainly have applied. I must leave you now. We have hospital patients to bring back from temporary exodus.'

I grabbed his hand and shook it. 'Thanks for everything, Doctor.'

'My pleasure,' he said and left the ward.

'Is there any hope for the others on the moon?' asked Linda.

'We're working on it,' said Neil. 'Now we know which radiation kills them, we'll soon find a way to apply it.'

'You need to do that before they find a way to get here, avoiding the Van Allen belts.' I said.

'Plans are afoot. We need you to be fighting fit and ready for the recovery mission,' said Neil.

'You want us to go back?' I asked in surprise.

'Well, only you. Linda's grounded,' said Neil.

I looked at her querulously.

'Firstly, we need you to concentrate on your recovery, then we're sending an expedition to recapture our Moonbase. We want our moon back!' said Neil.

'What about the Chinese base?' I asked.

'The Chinese are already on their way back to Earth. When we return to the moon, it will be a joint mission. Russia, China and the USA. Most will be military and medical, but you'll be our control subject. There's no substitute for experience,' said Neil. 'But I'll leave you now and let you rest. The sooner you're better, the sooner we can get rid of these entities permanently.'

We shook hands and Neil walked away along the ward, leaving Linda and I alone again.

'Why are you grounded? Was it the shortcuts?' I asked.

'Well, yes, in a sense it was. I picked up another hitch-hiker in orbit,' she said.

I looked at her strangely. 'What? You got infected too? How?'

'It was a shortcut *you* took, not *me*!' she said, then laughed.

'Eh?'

'Remember on the LOP? The things we didn't have with us because we left Moonbase in such a hurry?'

'What are you on about?'

'No condoms, stupid!'

Realisation dawned. 'You're pregnant?'

'Apparently. The tiniest trace of human chorionic gonadotropin was found when they examined me. I'm about seven days pregnant! We'll know for sure next week,' she said with a face-splitting smile.

'That's wonderful,' I said. I knew we'd fallen in love and we'd already spoken of marriage.

'We can move in together. If you want?' she said, leaning over to kiss me.

'I want!' I said and squeezed her hand.

'Permanent?'

'Oh, yes! Permanent.'

'Seriously?'

'We can get married, if you like,' I said.

She stood up defiantly with her hands on her hips. 'And what the hell sort of proposal is that?' she exclaimed.

I laughed. 'Sorry. Darling, Linda, will you do me the honour of becoming my wife?' I said, sitting up to meet her hugs and kisses halfway.

'It'll only be a seven-day honeymoon, Mark. Neil says you'll be blasting off at the end of the month and there's training to undertake.'

'We'd better find an available preacher or a ship's captain right away, then!' I said, and we kissed.

∞∞∞∞∞∞∞∞∞∞∞∞∞∞∞∞∞∞∞∞

So ends the beginning. Join Mark Noble on the next expedition – the battle to possess the moon in *MOONSTRUCK*. Sign up for the newsletter below to be advised when it's released.

A Word from Tony

Thank you for reading *MOONSCAPE*. Reviews are very important for authors and I wonder if I could ask you to say a few words on the review page where you purchased the book. Every review, even if it is only a few words with a star rating, helps the book move up the Amazon rankings.

Tony's Books

Currently, Tony has written five science fiction stories. Federation is the first of a trilogy and Moonscape is the first in a series about astronaut Mark Noble. You can find them all at https://harmsworth.net

THE DOOR*:* Henry Mackay and his dog regularly walk alongside an ancient convent wall. Today, as he passes the door, he glances at its peeling paint. Moments later he stops dead in his tracks. He returns to the spot, and all he sees is an ivy-covered wall. The door has vanished!

He unwittingly embarks on an exciting trail of events with twists, turns, quantum entanglement and temporal anomalies. It becomes an unbelievable adventure to save humanity which you'll be unable to put down.

The Door is an intriguing and unique science fiction mystery from the pen of Tony Harmsworth, the First Contact specialist who writes in the style of the old masters.

Discover the astonishing secrets being concealed by The Door today!

FEDERATION takes close encounters to a whole new level. A galactic empire of a quarter of a million worlds stumbles across the Earth. With elements of a political thriller, there is an intriguing storyline which addresses the environmental and social problems faced by the world today.

The aliens' philosophy on life is totally unexpected. With the help of intelligent automatons, they've turned what many on Earth felt was a reviled political system into a utopia for the masses, but are they a force for good or evil, and will the wealthy make the compromises needed for a successful outcome?

A Daragnen university graduate, Yol Rummy Blin Breganin, discovers that Earth failed in its attempt to join the Federation, and, for some unknown reason, members are forever banned from visiting or contacting the planet. Rummy had never heard of a whole world being outlawed. Perhaps it would be sensible to leave well enough alone but no, he decides to investigate…

FEDERATION is the first in a trilogy of near-future, hard science-fiction novels by *Tony Harmsworth*, the *First Contact* specialist.

Submerge yourself in humankind's cultural and economic dilemma. Buy *FEDERATION* today then the next two books, **FEDERATION & EARTH**, and **HIDDEN FEDERATION**.

MINDSLIP: The radiation from a nearby supernova causes every creature on Earth to swap minds! Men to women, children to adults, animals to humans, old to young, and vice versa. How would you handle changing sex or species? Mindslip combines frightening science fiction with psychological anguish.

The change in astrophysicist Geoff Arnold is challenging, and his wife and children have vanished. He joins the government's catastrophe committee with the brief to find a solution to *Mindslip* before it completely destroys society and the economy.

Millions die! Billions survive danger, harassment and abuse, and manage to adapt to their change of species, race, sex, and age. Geoff discovers that the change his wife has experienced is life-threatening. Can he juggle his new life, help save the world and rescue his wife in time?

This stand-alone work is an excellent example of Tony Harmsworth's imagination. Science fiction with elements of soft horror, all in the style of the old masters. A real page-turner.

Become part of the bizarre, yet realistic world of *MINDSLIP*. Buy it today!

MOONSCAPE: We've known that the moon is dead since Apollo. But what if something lay dormant in the dust, waiting to be found?

In 2028, Mark Noble is conducting a survey of a moon crater. The entity secretly grabs a ride back to Moonbase on Mark's buggy. Once in the habitat, it begins to infect the crew. They find themselves in a frightening, helter-skelter adventure with only two possible outcomes: losing or saving the Earth.

MOONSCAPE is the first in a series of hard science fiction stories featuring Mark Noble from the pen of Tony Harmsworth, a First Contact specialist who writes in the style of the old masters. If you like fast-paced adventure, fraught with the additional dangers found in space, then Tony's latest tale has been written especially for you.

Now read the sequel - ***MOONSTRUCK***

THE VISITOR: Specialist astronaut Evelyn Slater encounters a small, badly damaged, ancient, alien artefact on the first ever space-junk elimination mission. Where was it from? Who sent it?

International governments impose a security clampdown. Evelyn leads a team of hand-picked scientists who make amazing discoveries within the alien device. Secrecy becomes impossible to maintain. When the news is finally released, she becomes embroiled in international politics, worldwide xenophobic hatred and violence.

This is book one of Tony Harmsworth's First Contact series of novels. If you like realistic near-future stories which compel you to imagine yourself as the protagonist, The Visitor is the book for you.

THE VISITOR – hard science fiction with a wicked twist. Buy it now and be transported into orbit.

Non-Fiction by Tony Harmsworth

Loch Ness, Nessie & Me: Almost everyone, at some point in their lives, has wondered if there was any truth in the stories of monsters in Loch Ness? *Loch Ness, Nessie & Me* answers all the questions you have ever wanted to ask about the loch and its legendary beast.

In these 400 pages with more than **200 pictures and illustrations**, you will find a geography of Loch Ness; a travel guide to the area; a biography of its mythical inhabitant; and an autobiography of the man who set up the Loch Ness Centre, worked with many of the research groups, and helped coordinate Operation Deepscan.

Explore the environmental and physical attributes of Loch Ness which make certain monster candidates impossible. Find detailed explanations of how pictures were faked and sonar charts, badly interpreted. Learn how Nessie has affected the people and businesses which exist in her wake, and suspend belief over the activities of the monstrous monks of Fort Augustus Abbey.

Tony Harmsworth's involvement at the Loch has lasted over forty years, having created increasingly sceptical exhibitions, dioramas and multi-media shows. This is the first comprehensive book to be penned by someone who lives overlooking the loch. It is essential for anyone interested in Loch Ness and the process of analysing cryptozoological evidence.

Now's the time to discover the truth about this mystery, once and for all. Get your copy today!

Scotland's Bloody History: Ever been confused about Scotland's history – all the relationships between kings and queens, both Scottish and English? Why all the battles, massacres and disputes? *Scotland's Bloody History* simplifies it all.

Discover the history of Scotland from prehistoric man to the current Scottish Nationalist government. Follow the time-line from the stone-age, through the bronze age and the iron age. Find out about the Picts, the Scots, the Vikings and the English. Learn about the election of Scotland's early kings and how Shakespeare maligned one of its finest monarchs.

In simple, chronological order, this book will show you how the animosity between England and Scotland grew into outright warfare including tales of Braveheart and wars of independence.

Tony Harmsworth has taken the bloodiest events of the last three thousand years and used those to clarify the sequence of events. Don't buy this book to learn the boring stuff, this book is packed with action from page one to the final three words which might haunt you over the next decade.

Robert the Bruce, Mary Queen of Scots, the Stewarts and Jacobites. It is all there. Explore Scotland's Bloody History now!

Tony Harmsworth's Reader Club

Building a relationship with my readers is the very best thing about being a novelist. In these days of the internet and email, the opportunities to interact with you is unprecedented. I send occasional newsletters which include special offers and information on how the series are developing. You can keep in touch by signing up for my no-spam mailing list.

Sign up at my webpage: https://Harmsworth.net or on my Facebook.com/TonyHarmsworthAuthor and you will know when my books are released and will get free material from time to time and other information.

If you have questions, don't hesitate to write to me at Tony@Harmsworth.net.

Printed in Poland
by Amazon Fulfillment
Poland Sp. z o.o., Wrocław